PENGUIN CLASSICS

THE PILGRIM'S PROGRESS

John Bunyan (1628–88) was born at Elstow near Bedford. The son of a brazier, he learned to read and write at the village school and prepared to follow his father's trade. But in 1644, the Civil War changed the course of events and, at the age of sixteen, he was drafted into the Parliamentary army and was stationed at Newport Pagnell, from 1644 to 1646. In 1649, he married his first wife, by whom he had four children. She died *c.* 1656, and about three years later he married his second wife, Elizabeth.

It was in 1648 that Bunyan suffered a severe religious crisis which lasted for several years. He emerged with the resolution to convert others and help them in their spiritual problems. In 1653 he joined a Nonconformist church in Bedford, where he came into contact with the Quakers, against whom he published his first writings, *Some Gospel Truths Opened* (1656) and *A Vindication* (1657). In November 1660, he was arrested while preaching in the fields. He refused to cease preaching and spent most of the next twelve years in Bedford gaol. During the first half of this period, he wrote nine books and among them were *The Holy City, or the New Jerusalem* (1665), which was inspired by a passage in the book of Revelation, and his most well-known book of this period, *Grace Abounding to the Chief of Sinners* (1666), his spiritual autobiography. It centres almost wholly on the development of his inner religious feelings and in it he also describes his religious crisis of 1648. During the latter years of his imprisonment, Bunyan also began *The Pilgrim's Progress*, the work for which he is most famous, and which renders the personal spiritual experience of the earlier *Grace Abounding* into the more objective form of a universal myth, where all Christians who seek the truth are embodied within the figure of the solitary man pursuing his pilgrimage. In 1672, after his release from prison, he became pastor of the Bedford separatist church, but was imprisoned again in 1676 for a shorter period of about six months, during which he probably finished the first part of *The Pilgrim's Progress*, which was published in 1678. The second part, together with the whole work, was published in 1684. His other works include *The Life and Death of Mr Badman* (1680) and *The Holy War* (1682). He died just when the period of religious persecution was coming to an end.

Roger Sharrock is Emeritus Professor of English in the University of London where he held the chair at King's College; he has been Chairman of the English Association. Among other books and articles he is the author of the critical study *John Bunyan* and of *Saints, Sinners and Comedians*, on the novels of Graham Greene; he is the editor of the first volume of *The Pelican Book of English Prose* and general editor of the Oxford edition of *The Miscellaneous Works of John Bunyan*.

THE
PILGRIM'S PROGRESS

JOHN BUNYAN

Edited with an introduction and notes by
Roger Sharrock

PENGUIN BOOKS

PENGUIN BOOKS

Published by the Penguin Group
27 Wrights Lane, London W8 5TZ, England
Viking Penguin Inc., 40 West 23rd Street, New York, New York 10010, USA
Penguin Books Australia Ltd, Ringwood, Victoria, Australia
Penguin Books Canada Ltd, 2801 John Street, Markham, Ontario, Canada L3R 1B4
Penguin Books (NZ) Ltd, 182–190 Wairau Road, Auckland 10, New Zealand

Penguin Books Ltd, Registered Offices: Harmondsworth, Middlesex, England

This edition first published by the Penguin English Library 1965
Reprinted in Penguin Classics 1986
Reprinted with revisions 1987
5 7 9 10 8 6

Introduction copyright © Penguin Books Ltd, 1965, 1987
All rights reserved

Printed and bound in Great Britain by
Cox & Wyman Ltd, Reading
Set in Monotype Bembo

CONTENTS

INTRODUCTION

THE PILGRIM'S PROGRESS is a book which in the three hundred years of its existence has crossed most of those barriers of race and culture that usually serve to limit the communicative power of a classic. It has penetrated into the non-Christian world; it has been read by cultivated Moslems during the rise of religious individualism within Islam, and at the same time in cheap missionary editions by American Indians and South Sea Islanders. Its uncompromising evangelical Protestantism has not prevented it from exercising an appeal in Catholic countries. But to English readers it is bound to appear as the supreme classic of the English Puritan tradition. John Bunyan, its author, wrote about sixty other evangelical and controversial tracts; only three of his books are works of fiction, and of these only *The Pilgrim's Progress* has carried the heroic image of militant Puritanism to a vastly wider public than Bunyan's original Nonconformist audiences.

In literature, no less than in religion, Bunyan has always offended the establishment. The appeal of his coarse, speech-patterned English is not polite; he breaks the canon, and in a period which has become aware of the social limitations of the canon and the need to revise it, it is not surprising that there is a renewal of interest in his work. Indeed there is in progress an outburst of critical and scholarly activity comparable to that called forth in the Romantic age. The first complete edition of his writings is under way. The anniversary of his masterpiece occasioned a volume of essays on his narrative methods (*The Pilgrim's Progress: Critical and Historical Essays*, ed. Vincent Newey, Liverpool University Press, 1980);

he has been subjected to an early brand of the technique of deconstruction (Stanley Fish, *Self-Consuming Artifacts*, 1972); not unnaturally, for one in so sensitive a relation to his public, as preacher and fabulist, he has caught the attention of the founder of reader-response criticism (Wolfgang Iser, *The Implied Reader from Bunyan to Beckett*, 1974). The Marxists have begun to pay attention to his insights into a working-class world. But the predominantly and avowedly feminine world of the Second Part of *The Pilgrim's Progress* still awaits adequate attention. Meanwhile Christopher Hill and others have been exploring the background of radical Puritanism, flowering between 1640 and 1660, which formed the seed-bed for all his work.

The life of the author was as much a classic witness to that heroic Puritan faith as was the book; and though the book is a religious allegory in form, it grew naturally out of the circumstances of his life. Bunyan was born at Elstow near Bedford in 1628; he came of yeoman stock, but the family fortunes had declined and his father was a brazier or travelling tinker. He learned to read and write at a local grammar school and prepared to follow his father's trade. But in 1644 the Civil War swept him up into its course: at the age of sixteen he was mustered in the county levy, or militia, on the Parliamentary side, and spent some years on garrison duty before his discharge. Soon after this he married. His wife and he set up house 'as poor as poor might be, with not so much household-stuff as a dish or spoon betwixt us both'. About 1648 he was plunged into a religious crisis which lasted for several years and which brought him to the brink of despair. His vivid imagination was possessed in a simple and terrible form by the Calvinist doctrine that all men were predestined either to salvation or to damnation; he battled with doubts of his own faith. In *Grace Abounding to the Chief of Sinners* he has left an account of the fearful dreams and visions of this period: they took on the almost tangible form of voices, blows, and buffets, and he records the sensation of being pulled and pinched by the demons sent to torment him and the menacing texts of Scripture that filled his thoughts.

Weathering the storm, he emerged a new man after conversion, directed outwards to converting others and comforting them in their spiritual problems. He attached himself to a Nonconformist group in Bedford and began to preach. His new strength and resolution were soon put to the test, for in November 1660, a few months after Charles II's Restoration, he was arrested by a local magistrate while preaching in the fields. He refused to give an undertaking not to preach and was imprisoned off and on for the next twelve years. It seems that at any time he might have obtained his release: he had only to enter into a bond giving assurance that he would cease from preaching and evangelizing and conform to the worship of the Church of England. It is a measure of the personal integrity he had achieved that he refused to do this. His confinement was not brutal by twentieth-century standards, but like Boethius in the dungeon of the Gothic King, or like a modern political prisoner, he was put to the supreme existential test; isolated among people who believed that his conduct was foolish or criminal or both, he had to give a reason for the faith that was in him. This involved an examination of his past experience and a translation of it into a form which would

9

provide a recognizable pattern of hope for other Christians. Out of this grew his spiritual autobiography, *Grace Abounding to the Chief of Sinners*, and later *The Pilgrim's Progress* which renders the personal spiritual experience of the earlier book into the objective form of a universal myth. All types of Christians searching for the truth and prepared to reject a hostile society are comprehended under the figure of the wayfaring man earnestly pursuing his pilgrimage.

After his twelve years' imprisonment and another, shorter period of confinement, Bunyan became the pastor of the Bedford separatist church. He earned the nickname of 'Bishop Bunyan' for his zeal in travelling throughout Bedfordshire and into Cambridgeshire, both to preach and to attempt to solve the personal problems of his scattered congregation. He died in 1688 just when the period of religious persecution was drawing to an end and Nonconformists were becoming more fully integrated into the life of the nation.

The legend persisted down to recent times that Bunyan wrote *The Pilgrim's Progress* in the little town lock-up which stood in Bedford on the bridge over the Ouse till 1765. This was no place for a long imprisonment; in any case, Bunyan's was a county offence and would be punished in the county jail.* However, that he wrote the allegory in his prison is supported by the text: the book begins: 'As I walked through the wilderness of this world, I lighted on a certain place, where was a den; and I laid me down in that place to sleep'; and a note in the margin glosses 'den' as 'the gaol'. The sleeper recounts his dream,

* See Joyce Godber, *Transactions of the Congregational Historical Society*, vol. xvi (1949).

and half way through it he says, 'Then I awoke and dreamed again'. This suggests that Bunyan had obtained his release from prison before completing the book. Earlier students of Bunyan, like John Brown,* believed that *The Pilgrim's Progress* had been partly composed during the second shorter imprisonment of about six months. But a balance of recent opinion has inclined to the view that the work was begun during the first imprisonment, immediately after *Grace Abounding* was finished. It has the urgency, the air of absorbed self-discovery, that hangs about a prison book; and it is easy to see how its allegory builds on the first-hand experience of the autobiography.

Grace Abounding deals almost wholly with the development of his inner religious feelings; there are hardly any references to persons or places. Bunyan discards any attempts at literary adornment in order to achieve an absolutely naked rendering of his spiritual history. When there is an image it is drawn naturally from his life as a countryman: 'Down I fell as a bird that is shot from the tree,' he says when describing his surrender to the temptation of despair. But the effort to describe with complete honesty his inner psychological terrors, and his subsequent triumph over them, led him to the bold use of personification, since his terrors were so real and palpable. Voices urge him to blasphemy; threatening texts of Scripture 'do pinch him very sore' or 'lay like a mill-post upon his back'. *The Pilgrim's Progress* gives a further turn to this drive towards personification: Bunyan, the sole character of the autobiography, is now Christian, the spiritual pilgrim, but

* *John Bunyan: His Life, Times and Work* (1885, revised edition 1928).

instead of the empty introspective space of *Grace Abounding*, there is a peopled world for the hero to move through. The menacing texts become real demons to threaten his progress, the temptation to despair of his faith, which seems to have been the weakness Bunyan feared most, becomes a Giant Despair who locks him in his dungeon, and the reliance on the literal text of the Bible which is the prime motive of the autobiography is rendered by a character called Evangelist who reappears from time to time to guide a bewildered Christian back on to the road to the Celestial City.

The movement into allegory serves to naturalize and familiarize Bunyan's religious perceptions to us. As men and women and spiritual beings encountered along the road, his doubts and assurances lose some of the almost psychopathic intensity with which they are endowed in the autobiography; they cease to be peculiarities of Bunyan's temperament and become the doubts and assurances of the spirit that all of us feel from time to time. The process of changing his experience into fiction had led him to a less personal and more universal truth. But *The Pilgrim's Progress* still retains the sense of personal urgency: it is his tremendous need to find a righteousness not his own by which to be saved that we encounter in the very first paragraph, and which is the force irresistibly driving Christian along the road to his final entry into the Celestial City:

As I walked through the wilderness of this world, I lighted on a certain place, where was a den; and I laid me down in that place to sleep: and as I slept I dreamed a dream. I dreamed, and behold I saw a man clothed with rags, standing in a certain place, with his face from his own house, a book in his hand, and a great burden upon his back. I looked, and saw him open the book, and read therein; and as he read, he wept and trembled: and not being able longer to contain, he brake out with a lamentable cry saying, 'What shall I do?'

The naturalness of *The Pilgrim's Progress* springs from the fact that, while stressing the supreme importance of religious salvation according to the tenets of Bunyan and his immediate public, the book contrives to describe the familiar behaviour of people as we know them. This is not so paradoxical as it seems. Man is a creature who finds his own greatness in conforming to projects that lie beyond the attainment of material well-being. *The Pilgrim's Progress* describes in living examples the depths of hypocrisy and self-deceit and the splendours of martyrdom, and both are demonstrated in other creeds as well as Calvinism.

Coleridge could not grant that Calvinist theology had anything to do with Bunyan's success; he declared that 'His piety was baffled by his genius; and Bunyan the dreamer overcame the Bunyan of the conventicle'. Calvinism has gained an ill reputation for intolerance and bigotry, but it provided Bunyan and other Puritan Englishmen of his time with a powerful and dramatic myth: life was a confrontation between the powers of light and the powers of darkness, or, to change the metaphor, the adventurous journey of the armed and vigilant Christian through hostile country. As a pamphlet writer of the time, John Geree, says of the typical Puritan:

His whole life he accounted a warfare wherein Christ was his Captaine, his armes, prayers and teares, the Crosse his Banner . . .

Coleridge may indeed have underestimated the psychological dynamic of Calvinism and the manner in which its dramatic character could contribute something to a work of the imagination. But on the other hand it was undoubtedly valuable for Bunyan that he had not been born into a sectarian group, but had grown up as a typical member of an early seventeenth-century village community, not marked off from his fellows by any special claims to piety. Baulked in their bid for ecclesiastical power, the Puritan party had, between the Elizabethan Church Settlement and the Civil Wars, achieved a different kind of success: through their Calvinistic preaching and commenting on the English Bible they had effected a cultural revolution and created a new type of Englishman, endowed with an earnestness and a sense of mission not present in his medieval ancestor but familiar in the evangelical rebels and pioneers of the eighteenth and nineteenth centuries. Puritanism has been misconceived as restrictive moral prohibitions, weighed down by sexual guilt; in the mid seventeenth century it was a fiery religious and social dynamic resembling contemporary Marxism more than modern Fundamentalism. Bunyan's advantage was that as a convert he could draw both on the spirit of militant Puritanism and on the older traditions of figurative sermon and moral anecdote that linked the nineteenth-century village pulpit with medieval habits of preaching; for example with the personified 'Deadly Sins' in the preaching of the friars.

The keynote of the whole First Part of the book is this lonely integrity of the ideal Puritan; Christian is the central figure. The story begins when, at the prompting of Evangelist, he puts wife and children and security behind him and flies from their pleading with his fingers in his ears, crying, 'Life, life, eternal life'. His sole desire is to be on the right road to the Celestial City: 'he went like one that was all the while treading on forbidden ground, and could by no means think himself safe, till again he was got into the way'. From the start we are made to see everything from Christian's point of view, so that his desperate plight is humanly touching and convincing: we accept even his abandonment of his family because in the terms of the allegory their city is the City of Destruction, and Christian does his best to persuade them to leave it with him. As in Kafka's novels, we are placed in the situation of the central character and accept the world around him with complete objectivity whatever intensity of nightmare it inflicts. An overhanging mountain (Mount Sinai representing the old law of sin and death) threatens to fall upon Christian with peals of thunder; a little later he has to endure foul smoke, demons, whisperings, and blasphemies in the Valley of the Shadow of Death (recalling Bunyan's own worst temptations). But this allegory of the darker side of Calvinist spiritual experience is not allowed to become morbidly subjective; Bunyan sets his own experience in an inhabited world, and by so doing draws it nearer to the experience of other Christian people so that it appears less as a special and obsessed phenomenon than it does in the revelations of *Grace Abounding*.

For instance, early on his pilgrimage Christian encounters Worldly-Wiseman who meets him with pompous self-assurance: 'How now, good fellow, whither away after this burdened manner?' Wiseman attempts to convince him that he will save himself a great deal of trouble by adopting a merely nominal and respectable form of Christianity. This is expressed in the allegory by an invitation to take up residence in the village of Morality under the care of Legality and his son Civility: 'Provision is there also cheap and good, and that which will make thy life the more happy, is, to be sure there thou shalt live by honest neighbours, in credit and good fashion.' In the strict terms of the allegory Mr Worldly-Wiseman stands for the temptation of the World and provides a satirical comment on the attractions of a merely conformist, 'Establishment' type of Christianity. But he appears in the narrative as a living personality, talking and acting for himself the role of a pompous humbug, the eternal bourgeois trying to tell a social inferior the way he should go ('Hast thou a wife and children?').

The strength of the work and the sense of reality it communicates to readers of widely differing varieties of belief depend on this combination of religious vision with loving, exact observation of human character.

The presentation of characters is often most lively in the studies of hypocrites and villains met along the way; By-Ends is a near relation of Worldly-Wiseman and his corruption is suggested by a similar air of social importance with which he invests himself.

My wife is a very virtuous woman, the daughter of a virtuous woman. She was my Lady Faining's daughter, therefore she came of a very honourable family, and is arrived to such a pitch of breeding, that she knows how to carry it to all, even to prince and peasant. 'Tis true, we somewhat differ in religion from those of the stricter sort . . .

But insight into the natural processes of human intercourse is not confined to the satirical portraits. Christian's companions along the road, Faithful and, after his martyrdom, Hopeful, tend to be less strongly characterized than the tempters; they do however afford an opportunity for some moving instances of the beauty of friendship; again, all of them ring psychologically true. Before ever he meets Faithful, Christian knows that he is going before him through the Valley of the Shadow of Death, and is encouraged in his own lonely ordeal when he hears the unknown friend-to-be singing out, 'Though I walk through the Valley of the Shadow of Death, I will fear none ill, for thou art with me'. Before the heroic endurance of his martyrdom at Vanity Fair, Faithful is little more than a peg on which to hang a doctrinal summary of the action in the form of dialogue between him and Christian; later the relationship of Christian with Hopeful is developed with more subtlety. Hopeful is young and untried, the tyro to Christian, now an experienced pilgrim. But Christian is always falling through unpreparedness and it is at his careless instigation that Hopeful lets himself be persuaded to take a short cut by By-Path Meadow which leads them eventually into the hands of Giant Despair. At first Hopeful cannot help the universal human urge to say 'I told you so': 'I was afraid on't at very first ... I would have spoke plainer, but that you are older than I'. Christian apologizes handsomely; so far, both moral lesson and realistic observation of character are straightforward. But then each strives to excel the other in a bravery that is also sensitive. Christian wishes to go first on the dangerous path because it is on his account they are in it; Hopeful, with a fine sense of discretion, declares he must not do so, 'for your mind being troubled may lead you out of the way again'. This is clearly a realism that can explore human affection as well as human faith.

For the same reasons the allegory of *The Pilgrim's Progress* is not intellectual or highly organized as in the sophisticated religious allegory of Dante or

Spenser. Many of the figures and incidents that spring up along the route are created for the sake of an immediate effect and then passed over when a fresh incident occurs in Christian's progress; they are not closely related to the main structure of the allegory. Such are many of the personages who are simply mentioned for the effect of their names. (Bunyan is extremely skilful with names: consider those of the packed jury at Faithful's trial: 'Mr Blind-man, Mr No-good, Mr Malice, Mr Love-lust, Mr Live-loose, Mr Heady, Mr High-mind, Mr Enmity, Mr Liar, Mr Cruelty, Mr Hate-light, and Mr Implacable'.) In the same way the allegory is not consistently maintained; realism is always breaking in, because the one truly binding element in the structure of the narrative is Christian's drive onward through dangerous country to the Celestial City, and the stream of adventures that he encounters as a pilgrim. Thus the metaphor of warfare against the powers of darkness is generally kept up ('put on you the whole armour of God'): Christian fights Apollyon, the demon of spiritual doubt, with sword in hand and armour on his back. But as he goes on with drawn sword through the demon-haunted valley we are told that 'he was forced to put up his sword, and betake himself to another weapon called All-prayer; so he cried, in my hearing, "O Lord I beseech thee deliver my soul"'. Bunyan has simply slipped out of the allegorical mode and declared directly that prayer is the chief weapon against temptation. Such apparent clumsiness does not result in any failure of interest, still less in any breakdown of the primary illusion of fiction. This is not solely due to the often real charm of Bunyan's naïveté when he is making such *gaffes*. If Bunyan is blundering here, he is blundering with his eye on the object and avoiding

18

the mistakes of an over-classified and mechanical spiritual allegory. The thrill of struggle remains, and with it the illusion of a dramatic fiction, because though there may be a departure from a uniform allegorical framework, the metaphors are still there embedded in all human thinking about this type of experience. Prayer is still 'another weapon'. In the same way, characters appear not as the perfect, digested essences of a certain quality, but as that quality in action in a human being. The simple and modest veteran Honest in the Second Part says, 'Not honesty in the abstract, but Honest is my name, and I wish that my nature shall agree to what I am called'.

For the modern reader, the human working compromise between realism and allegory is likely to conceal the firm outlines of the theological structure which were much more obvious to Bunyan's contemporaries and especially to his fellow-Nonconformists. What is on the surface an episodic series of adventures, a narrative of folk-tale ups and downs such as Bunyan himself enjoyed in the popular romances of his unregenerate youth, has a tough skeleton of which each articulated joint precisely indicates a stage in the Puritan psychology of conversion. There is conviction of sin, classically accepted as the first awakening of the soul; this is represented by Christian's leaving the City of Destruction at the beginning, only to fall into the Slough of Despond. The episode of Worldly-Wiseman deals briefly and effectively with the next stage: the attempt to found the religious life on moral righteousness, inevitably doomed to failure. Then comes the gradual education of the convert through Bible-study and meditation; Christian is entertained at the House of the Interpreter by a series of emblematic pictures. As with the popular romances like *The Seven Champions of Christendom*, Bunyan here draws imaginative life from another folk form, the emblem books with their combined mottoes, verses, and symbolic illustrations (it was originally a learned form, but by the late seventeenth century had come down in the world, from the cabinet of the Renaissance humanist to the children's reading book aimed at a middle-class public).

Christian then comes to the Cross where the burden (of his original sin) that he has been carrying falls from his shoulder and is buried in the open sepulchre below. Again there is a mixture of fresh allegorical invention with the traditional symbols of the Redemption, and indeed with the dramatic features of the Gospel story. Christian is clothed in white raiment, a mark is set on his forehead, and he is given the roll of his salvation. It might seem, with two-thirds of the story to go, that the narrative was here in danger of succumbing to the remorseless mechanics of the Calvinist doctrine of conversion. Christian has received an assurance of grace; he is numbered among the elect, among those who are to be saved from damnation. But many of the most desperate adventures with the forces of doubt and despair lie ahead: this is not the end of the drama but the beginning. God may have chosen Christian, but the reader sees this only as something seen by Christian, an assurance strong at the time but likely to become weaker under fresh assaults of temptation and when the moment of grace is past. However simple his techniques and attitudes, in this respect Bunyan writes as a man of the new post-Cartesian age for whom the world of religious fact, like the physical world, is something lying apart from his own consciousness and having to be perceived through it.

The narrative now proceeds by alternating scenes of exciting action and static recuperation at various houses of resort for pilgrims along the road. Sometimes the quiet rests in the story are provided by doctrinal and moral conservation between Christian and the other pilgrims. Thus the story-teller's need for action and relief from action is combined with the need to incorporate some overtly didactic matter into a fable that must have seemed extraordinarily daring in its time (it offended many members of Bunyan's sect). In the House Beautiful there is more education through symbols and preparation for future dangers; but the chief impression conveyed by the women who tend Christian there is of the human dignity of the best English Puritan household rather than of vague female allegorical personages: Piety and Prudence they may be called, but these very names take us into the middle-class families of Bunyan's time. After this Christian is ready to meet the terrors of the Valley of Humiliation and the Valley of the Shadow of Death.

United for a time with Faithful, Christian and he engage in a long argument with Talkative. Talkative can give a plausible imitation of having undergone the sort of religious experience shared by the two pilgrims. But their interrogation reveals that this is a façade: 'the soul of religion is the practic part'; the most evident sign of grace is the transformation of the ordinary moral life, and of this Talkative knows nothing. He is one of several types of hypocrite encountered on the pilgrimage; their exposure does more than provide comic relief since it serves to base Christian's aspirations on the firm ground of daily living.

The pilgrims go on to Vanity-Fair. Here again the purely allegorical conception of a city to represent the attractions of worldly power and sensuality is strongly modified by contemporary reference and a complex of unconscious allusions; the Fair with its separate rows for the merchants of different nationalities recalls the great summer fairs of eastern England like that at Stourbridge, probably known to Bunyan. Once Christian and Faithful fall foul of the authorities, and are persecuted and then brought to trial, the atmosphere is that of a seventeenth-century English court applying the penal laws against Dissenters, but shot through with nightmarish evocations of the martyrdom of the early Christians as recounted in Foxe's *Acts and Monuments*. The bullying judge and the packed jury, the crowds mocking at the strange clothes of the prisoners, all these features speak straight to the problems of the English Nonconformist in the age of Judge Jeffreys; by so doing they give the grim episode an authenticity and hardness of outline that could never be obtained by pure allegorizing.

Christian escapes the fate of Faithful. After another static episode of conversation with backsliders from the town of Fair-speech, he and Hopeful, his new companion, fall into the hands of Giant Despair and are imprisoned in Doubting-Castle. The episode has a dramatic importance corresponding to the significance attached by Bunyan to the sin of spiritual despair; he had suffered himself from this gnawing doubt, the medieval *accidie*, and therefore ranked it above all the other dangers of the spiritual life. Christian is always falling through unpreparedness: immediately after a stroll by the River of the Water of Life, which has given him new ease of mind, he wanders into By-Path Meadow. Bunyan excels in depicting the particular price one pays for advantages gained.

After sojourning briefly with the shepherds among the evocatively named Delectable Mountains, Christian and Hopeful go on their way. The pilgrimage continues at a more leisurely pace; after all, the best narratives do not retain a constant momentum but sink away serenely towards the close. A series of static episodes of argument and conversation introduce some more hypocrites and backsliders, the glib and callow youth Ignorance and a group of time-servers, By-Ends and his companions. The skill with which whole depths of self-deception are suggested by a short answer to a question is masterly:

Ignorance. But my heart and life agree together, and therefore my hope is well grounded.
Christian. Who told thee that thy heart and life agrees together?
Ignorance. My heart tells me so.

After this, these quieter episodes shade gradually to the arrival of Hopeful and Christian in the land of Beulah, where the air is sweet and pleasant, and every day the flowers appear in the earth. Here is their resting place before their passage over the River of Death, and the finale. Though 'much stounded' at the River, they pass through its waters to the Celestial City, and the trumpets sound for them on the other side.

The Second Part of *The Pilgrim's Progress* was written six years after the first (1684) and is really an independent work. Christiana and her children decide to go on pilgrimage; she is sorry not to have accompanied her husband in the first place. They are escorted by the warrior Great-heart, an archetype of the ideal Puritan pastor. The pace is leisurely; sometimes it seems almost like a conducted tour of the battlefields where Christian vanquished giants and demons. Occasionally there is a giant-fight, but Great-heart now has sturdy supporters from the different houses of resort along the way, and the resulting combats resemble an afternoon's hunting rather than the life-and-death struggles of the First Part. There are even monumental inscriptions of Christian's triumphs to read along the way. But the work is no forced sequel: it is a different book, a bustling social novel. Christiana and her beloved friend Mercy may seem to be moving in the after-glow of her husband's heroism, but they have their own vitality. Mercy wards off an unwelcome suitor; the children grow up and get married; Christiana fusses, is tender, and endures to the end of the pilgrimage. The interest has shifted from the lonely epic of the individual to the problems of the small urban community of Nonconformists: problems of mixed marriages, the need for cohesion, and the difficulty certain members have (Fearing, Feeble-mind) in fitting into the life of the church. Bunyan had now been many years an administrator and a pastor of souls. Like Fielding in his days as a Bow Street magistrate writing fiction about the real nature of justice and crime in contemporary society, he now has a professional point of view from which to pass judgement. As most novelists do, he has passed from an autobiographical first novel to an external, more calculated subject.

The Pilgrim's Progress is soaked in the imagery of the Bible and deeply pervaded by the Puritan belief that the Bible provided a key to every problem of life and thought. But it would be a careless reading of the book that gave the impression that the Authorized Version was the main influence on Bunyan's style. His language has the life of speech, salted with proverbs and vigorous provincial turns of phrase; it is the plain colloquial manner that he no doubt also employed in the pulpit: 'his house is as empty of religion as the white of an egg is of savour'; 'we were as merry as the maids'; 'he all to-befooled me'. It is the manner of generations of popular preachers using parables to point their case, but in *The Pilgrim's Progress* it is wrought to the pitch of art. Many proverbs and phrases have gained a new life and continued in circulation on account of their use in the allegory.

The achievement of Bunyan in *The Pilgrim's Progress* which gives the work its continuing vitality is the creation, not of allegory, but of myth. Allegory is dependent on an intellectual scheme: we can connect symbol and significance neatly with an 'equals' sign, and for a purely allegorical work it should always be possible to compile a table of characters and meanings in two columns which should perform the whole work of commentary. Christian, young Ignorance, Great-heart, and the country through which they go, are not like this. Their moral significance cannot be neatly pared away from the sensuous form in which they are presented. This is something which is far easier to realize than to discuss, but there is one striking demonstration of the authenticity of Bunyan's fiction: each main episode has carried over into the sensibility of English-speaking people, many of whom have not read the book but have met its ideas through the floating mythology by which the life of a people is lived—Vanity-Fair, the Slough of Despond, the Delectable Mountains. The conception of Vanity-Fair is an imaginative shorthand for all the pride and show of the acquisitive life; its notion of a raree-show of human pride was the working model on which Thackeray could build his contemporary illustration of the myth. Sometimes

Bunyan's imagination is illuminating or recasting traditional symbols; the Christian warfare, waged with the protection of 'the whole armour of God', is one of these. The figure of the lonely wayfaring man, the simple, honest foot-traveller with his pack on his back, goes back to the middle ages; Langland's Piers Plowman sets out thus on pilgrimage to find Truth after he has ploughed his half-acre. The modern imagination perhaps tends to see man more as a prisoner than as a traveller, but the image of the purposeful journey through life still has great evocative power; it is reflected in all those long fictions of which the main theme is individual growth, from Proust to Anthony Powell and C. P. Snow.

Sometimes Bunyan develops a very slight metaphorical hint in Scripture into a fully-realized allegorical episode: the Valley of the Shadow of Death, with its deep ditch on one side and mire on the other, haunted by the same voices and noises as preyed on Bunyan in the days of his obsession with personal guilt, is an example of such free interpretation. The hint of a single figure of speech has been daringly expanded. Similarly, the friendliness and dignity of the houses of resort along the road owe much to the entertainment of Christians in apostolic times, as it is described in the Acts of the Apostles; again, hints have been exapnded into full-grown fictions. Clearly, if the Bible has not influenced the language of *The Pilgrim's Progress*, Bunyan's intense, peculiar reading of Scripture has guided the very structure of his narrative.

Literary criticism in our time has shown a refined preoccupation with the art of narrative. Among the reasons for the increase of interest in Bunyan may be the fact that most of the devices and problems of narrative come up in the course of *The Pilgrim's*

Progress. Every time Bunyan, in his sublime uncon-
sciousness, breaks the pattern of his own allegory, or
breaks the fiction by talking directly to the reader,
we see the mysteriousness of the fictional thing by
thus being distanced from it.

In his prefatory verses Bunyan uses a metaphor
from flax-spinning to suggest how effortlessly the
whole story came to him once he had started:

> Still as I pull'd, it came.

It is this sheer creative spontaneity of *The Pilgrim's
Progress*, drawing on the deepest resources of the
popular tradition and the unconscious mind, that
makes the book fascinating. A seventeenth-century
Calvinist sat down to write a tract and produced a
folk-epic of the universal religious imagination.

ROGER SHARROCK

A NOTE ON THE TEXT

THE PILGRIM'S PROGRESS was first published in 1678 by Nathaniel Ponder, 'at the Peacock in the Poultrey'; later as Bunyan's regular publisher he became known as 'Bunyan Ponder'. Second (1678) and third (1679) editions followed; these contained several additions including the whole episode of By-Ends and his companions. There were twelve editions in all in Bunyan's lifetime. The Second Part first appeared in 1684, and since then both parts have been published together.

A critical text was edited by J. B. Wharey (Oxford, 1928). In my revision of that edition (Oxford, 1960) a return was made to the first edition, restoring the original vigorous colloquial forms which were later modified by the printing-house. A similar plan has been followed in this edition, though spelling and punctuation have been modernized to meet the needs of the general reader. The use of capitals in the early editions was generous; in this edition capitals have been retained only in the case of personification and where their use is otherwise essential to the allegorical sense.

Chronology of Bunyan's Life

1628 John Bunyan was born at Elstow near Bedford, the eldest of three sons of Thomas Bunyan and his wife Margaret Bentley. The father was a brazier or tinker, poor but not a vagabond, sinced he owned a cottage between Elstow and Bedford.

c.1638 He attended for a time Bedford grammar school or that at Houghton Conquest nearby. He was taken from school to follow his father's trade.

1644 His mother died and his father married again within the year. In November he was mustered in a county levy of the Parliamentary army (the Civil War had been in progress for two years) and was assigned to the garrison at Newport Pagnell.

1645–6 He seems to have spent most of his military service in garrison duty and there is little support for the theory that he was present at the siege of Leicester in 1645.

1647 His company was disbanded and he returned to Elstow to practise his trade.

1649 He married his first wife 'whose Father was counted godly'.

1650 His blind daughter Mary was born. Three other children of the first marriage followed.

1650–4 He underwent the spiritual crisis described in *Grace Abounding*; in the course of it he came into contact with the Open Communion church in Bedford and its pastor John Gifford, an ex-Royalist officer.

1655 Having joined the Bedford church he discovered his gift in speaking to the brethren.

1656	He began to preach the Word in the neighbourhood. He became involved in disputes with the local Quakers under Edward Burrough; these led to his first book, *Some Gospel-Truths Opened*.
1658	His first wife died. In *A Few Sighs from Hell* he projected his recent terrors into an arousing sermon treatise.
1659	He married his second wife Elizabeth. *The Doctrine of the Law and Grace Unfolded*, his most ambitious theological work, was published.
1660	He is arrested for preaching to a conventicle (unauthorized religious service) at Lower Samsell. The persecution of Nonconformists had only just begun and the penal legislation of the Clarendon Code was yet to be enacted.
1661	He is tried and sentenced to three months' imprisonment in the county jail. Since he refused to give an assurance not to preach, he remained in prison for twelve years, but there were some short periods of parole and he attended some meetings of the Bedford church. During imprisonment he supported his family by making 'long tagged laces' for shoes.
1663	*Christian Behaviour*.
1665	*The Holy City*.
1666	*Grace Abounding*, his spiritual autobiography.
1667–72	In this period Bunyan probably wrote the First Part of *The Pilgrim's Progress*.
1672	He was elected pastor of the Bedford church and, in March, released from prison

under Charles II's first Declaration of Indulgence. From this point until his death he led a busy life preaching, directing the affairs of the church, and visiting outlying congregations outside Bedford and sister churches in London. It is now that he earned the nickname 'Bishop Bunyan'.

1677 He was imprisoned for six months early in the year.

1678 *The Pilgrim's Progress* (First Part).

1680 *The Life and Death of Mr Badman*.

1682 *The Holy War*.

1684 *The Pilgrim's Progress* (Second Part).

1685 He made a deed of gift of his property to his wife, probably to avoid confiscation during the period of renewed persecution.

1688 He died in London at the house of a friend, 31 August, after contracting a fever during a journey by horse from Reading to offer reconciliation in a family dispute. Buried in Bunhill Fields.

Suggestions for Further Reading

Works by Bunyan

The Works of That Eminent Servant of Christ Mr. John Bunyan, edited by Charles Doe (1692). This first collected edition in a single folio volume, by a printer who was a friend of Bunyan, is incomplete.

The Works of That Eminent Servant of Christ, Mr. John Bunyan, edited by Samuel Wilson (2 vols., 1736–7). The completion of the 1692 edition, often reprinted.

The Works of John Bunyan, edited by George Offor (3 vols., London and Edinburgh, 1806–2). The extensive commentary is unscholarly and stridently pious, but this is the last complete edition, and it is full of information.

The Miscellaneous Works of John Bunyan, edited by Roger Sharrock (Oxford University Press, 1976–). A complete text based on the earliest editions and with full introductions, critical apparatus, and historical and explanatory notes. Thirteen volumes, of which six have appeared. Uniform with the personal and allegorical works in four volumes.

Grace Abounding to the Chief of Sinners, edited by Roger Sharrock (Clarendon Press, 1962).

The Holy War, edited by Roger Sharrock and James F. Forrest (Clarendon Press, 1980).

The Life and Death of Mr Badman, edited by Roger Sharrock and James F. Forrest (Clarendon Press, to appear shortly).

The Pilgrim's Progress From This World To That Which Is To Come, edited by James Blanton Wharey and revised by Roger Sharrock (Clarendon Press, 1960, and subsequent reprints).

Grace Abounding and The Pilgrim's Progress, edited by Roger Sharrock (Oxford University Press, 1966).

The Puritan Background

Richard Baxter, *Reliquiae Baxterianae*, edited by Matthew Sylvester (1696; selections edited by J. M. Lloyd Thomas, Dent, 1925, etc.).

The Narrative of the Persecution of Agnes Beaumont in 1674, edited with an introduction by G. B. Harrison (Constable, 1929).

A Biographical Dictionary of British Radicals in the Seventeenth Century, edited by Richard L. Greaves and Robert Zaller (Harvester Press, 1981).

Calamy Revised, edited by A. G. Matthews (Oxford University Press, 1934). The lives of Puritan ministers ejected after the Restoration in 1662.

The Journeys of Celia Fiennes, edited by Christopher Morris (Cresset Press, 1947).

George Fox, *Journal*, revised edition by John L. Nickalls (Cambridge University Press, 1952).

Lucy Hutchinson, *Memoirs of Colonel Hutchinson*, edited by James Sutherland (Oxford University Press, 1973).

Revolutionary Prose of the English Civil War, edited by Howard Erskine-Hill and Graham Storey (Cambridge University Press, 1983).

The Puritans, edited by Perry Miller and T. H. Johnson (American Book Company, 1938). A useful collection of texts.

Modern Studies

Historical and Theological

Robert Barclay, *The Inner Life of the Religious Societies of the Commonwealth* (1876).

36

L. F. Brown, *Baptists and Fifth Monarchy Men during the Interregnum* (Clarendon Press, 1912).

Edward Dowden, *Puritan and Anglican* (Kegan Paul, 1900).

William Haller, *The Rise of Puritanism* (Columbia University Press, 1938).

William Haller, *Liberty and Reformation in the Puritan Revolution* (Columbia University Press, 1953).

Christopher Hill, *The Century of Revolution, 1603–1714* (Thomas Nelson, 1961).

Christopher Hill, *Puritanism and Revolution: Studies in Interpretation of the English Revolution of the Seventeenth Century* (Secker & Warburg, 1958).

N. H. Keeble, *Richard Baxter: Puritan Man of Letters* (Clarendon Press, 1982).

Geoffrey F. Nuttall, *The Holy Spirit in Puritan Faith and Experience* (Basil Blackwell, 1946).

Geoffrey F. Nuttall, *Visible Saints: The Congregational Way, 1640–1660* (Basil Blackwell, 1957).

Puritans and Revolutionaries: Essays on Seventeenth-Century History Presented to Christopher Hill, edited by Donald Pennington and Keith Thomas (Oxford University Press, 1978).

Robert S. Paul, *The Lord Protector: Religion and Politics in the Life of Oliver Cromwell* (Lutterworth Press, 1955).

Wilhelm Schenk, *The Concern for Social Justice in the Puritan Revolution* (Longmans, 1948).

R. H. Tawney, *Religion and the Rise of Capitalism* (John Murray, 1926, etc.).

Ernst Troeltsch, *The Social Teaching of the Christian Churches*, translated by Olive Wyon (Allen & Unwin, 1931).

Murray Tolmie, *The Triumph of the Saints* (Cambridge University Press, 1978).

G. S. Wakefield, *Puritan Devotion: Its Place in the Development of Christian Piety* (Epworth Press, 1957).

Owen C. Watkins, *The Puritan Experience* (Routledge & Kegan Paul, 1972). On spiritual autobiographies in the seventeenth century.

Michael Watts, *The Dissenters* (Oxford University Press, 1978).

C. E. Whiting, *Studies in English Puritanism, 1660–1688* (Society for Promoting Christian Knowledge, 1931).

Keith Wrightson, *English Society 1580–1680* (Longman, 1982).

Biographical and Literary

Jacques Blondel, *Allégorie et réalisme dans le Pilgrim's Progress* (Archives des Lettres Modernes, 1959).

John Brown, *John Bunyan: His Life, Times and Work* (1885; revised by F. M. Harrison, Hulbert Publishing Company, 1928).

Sir Charles Firth, *Essays Historical and Literary* (Clarendon Press, 1938).

R. M. Frye, *God, Man and Satan* (Princeton University Press, 1960).

Joyce Godber, 'The Imprisonments of John Bunyan', *Transactions of the Congregational Historical Society* vol. xvi (1949).

Richard L. Greaves, *John Bunyan* (Abingdon, 1969). A study of Bunyan's theology.

Sir Herbert Grierson, *Cross Currents in English Literature of the Seventeenth Century* (Chatto & Windus, 1927).

Gwilym O. Griffith, *John Bunyan* (Hodder & Stoughton, 1927).

F. M. Harrison, 'A Bibliography of the Works of

John Bunyan' *Supplement No. 6 to the Transactions of the Bibliographical Society* (Oxford, 1932).

G. B. Harrison, *John Bunyan: A Study in Personality* (Dent, 1928).

Maurice Hussey, in *The Pelican Guide to English Literature Vol. 3: From Donne to Marvell* (Penguin, 1956).

Wolfgang Iser, 'Bunyan's *Pilgrim's Progress*: die kalvinistische Heilsgewissheit und die Form des Romans', in *Festschrift für Walther Bülst* (Heidelberg, 1960).

U. M. Kaufmann, *The Pilgrim's Progress and Traditions in Puritan Meditation* (Yale University Press, 1966).

Arnold Kettle, in *The English Novel* (Hutchinson, 1951, etc.).

John R. Knott, Jr., in *The Sword of the Spirit: Puritan Responses to the Bible* (Chicago University Press, 1980).

F. R. Leavis, in *The Common Pursuit* (Chatto & Windus, 1952).

Bunyan's *The Pilgrim's Progress: Essays Historical and Literary*, edited by Vincent Newey (Liverpool University Press, 1980).

Roy Pascal, 'The Present Tense in *The Pilgrim's Progress*', *Modern Language Review* vol. lx (1965).

Mark Rutherford (William Hale White), *John Bunyan* (1905; new edition, Nelson, 1933).

Roger Sharrock, 'Personal Vision and Puritan Tradition in Bunyan', *Hibbert Journal* (1957).

Roger Sharrock, *The Pilgrim's Progress* (Arnold, 1966). Critical study.

The Pilgrim's Progress: A Casebook, edited and selected by Roger Sharrock (Macmillan, 1976).

George Bernard Shaw, from the Preface to *Man and*

Superman, in *Dramatic Opinions and Essays* (Constable, 1970).

Robert Southey, Introduction to his edition of *The Pilgrim's Progress* (1830; reprinted in *Select Biographies*, 1844).

Henri A. Talon, *John Bunyan, the Man and his Works* (Paris, 1948; English translation, Rockcliff, 1951).

Henri A. Talon, *John Bunyan* (Longman, 1956).

William York Tindall, *John Bunyan: Mechanick Preacher* (Columbia University Press, 1934).

Dorothy Van Ghent, in *The English Novel: Form and Function* (Rinehart, 1953).

Joan Webber, in *The Eloquent I: Style and Self in Seventeenth-Century Prose* (University of Wisconsin Press, 1968).

J. B. Wharey, *The Sources of Bunyan's Allegories* (J. H. Furst Company, 1904).

O. L. Winslow, *John Bunyan* (Macmillan, New York, 1961). A straightforward biography.

THE
Pilgrim's Progress
FROM
THIS WORLD,
TO
That which is to come:

Delivered under the Similitude of a

DREAM

Wherein is Discovered,
The manner of his setting out,
His Dangerous Journey; And safe
Arrival at the Desired Countrey.

I have used Similitudes, Hos. 12. 10.

By *John Bunyan.*

Licensed and Entred according to Order.

LONDON,
Printed for *Nath. Ponder* at the *Peacock*
in the *Poultrey* near *Cornhil,* 1678.

THE AUTHOR'S APOLOGY FOR
HIS BOOK

WHEN at the first I took my pen in hand,
    Thus for to write, I did not understand
    That I at all should make a little book
In such a mode; nay, I had undertook
To make another, which when almost done,
Before I was aware, I this begun.

    And thus it was: I writing of the way
And race of saints[1] in this our Gospel-day,
Fell suddenly into an allegory
About their journey, and the way to glory,
In more than twenty things, which I set down;
This done, I twenty more had in my crown,
And they again began to multiply,
Like sparks that from the coals of fire do fly.
Nay then, thought I, if that you breed so fast,
I'll put you by yourselves, lest you at last
Should prove *ad infinitum*, and eat out
The book that I already am about.

    Well, so I did; but yet I did not think
To show to all the world my pen and ink
In such a mode; I only thought to make
I knew not what, nor did I undertake
Thereby to please my neighbour; no, not I,
I did it mine own self to gratify.

    Neither did I but vacant seasons spend
In this my scribble, nor did I intend
But to divert myself in doing this,
From worser thoughts which make me do amiss.

    Thus I set pen to paper with delight,
And quickly had my thoughts in black and white.
For having now my method by the end,
Still as I pulled it came,[2] and so I penned
It down, until it came at last to be

For length and breadth the bigness which you see.
　　Well, when I had thus put mine ends together,
I show'd them others that I might see whether
They would condemn them, or them justify:
And some said, 'let them live'; some, 'let them die':
Some said, 'John, print it'; others said, 'not so':
Some said, 'it might do good'; others said, 'no'.
　　Now was I in a strait, and did not see
Which was the best thing to be done by me:
At last I thought, since you are thus divided,
I print it will, and so the case decided.
　　For, thought I, some I see would have it done,
Though others in that channel do not run.
To prove then who advised for the best,
Thus I thought fit to put it to the test.
　　I further thought, if now I did deny
Those that would have it thus, to gratify,
I did not know, but hinder them I might,
Of that which would to them be great delight.
　　For those that were not for its coming forth,
I said to them, offend you I am loth;
Yet since your brethren pleased with it be,
Forbear to judge, till you do further see.
　　If that thou wilt not read, let it alone;
Some love the meat, some love to pick the bone:
Yea, that I might them better palliate,
I did too with them thus expostulate.
　　May I not write in such a style as this?
In such a method too, and yet not miss
Mine end, thy good? why may it not be done?
Dark clouds bring waters, when the bright bring
　　　　none;
Yea, dark, or bright, if they their silver drops
Cause to descend, the earth by yielding crops
Gives praise to both, and carpeth not at either,
But treasures up the fruit they yield together:

44

Yea, so commixes both, that in her fruit
None can distinguish this from that, they suit
Her well when hungry, but if she be full
She spews out both, and makes their blessings null.

You see the ways the fisherman doth take
To catch the fish, what engines doth he make?
Behold! how he engageth all his wits
Also his snares, lines, angles, hooks and nets.
Yet fish there be, that neither hook, nor line,
Nor snare, nor net, nor engine can make thine;
They must be groped for, and be tickled too,
Or they will not be catched, what e'er you do.

How doth the fowler seek to catch his game?
By divers means, all which one cannot name.
His gun, his nets, his lime-twigs, light and bell:
He creeps, he goes, he stands; yea, who can tell
Of all his postures? Yet there's none of these
Will make him master of what fowls he please.
Yea, he must pipe, and whistle to catch this,
Yet if he does so, that bird he will miss.

If that a pearl may in a toad's head dwell,[3]
And may be found too in an oyster-shell;
If things that promise nothing, do contain
What better is than gold, who will disdain
(That have an inkling of it) there to look,
That they may find it? Now my little book
(Though void of all those paintings that may make
It with this or the other man to take)
Is not without those things that do excel,
What do in brave but empty notions dwell.

'Well, yet I am not fully satisfied,
That this your book will stand, when soundly
    tried.'

Why, what's the matter? 'It is dark', What tho'?
'But it is feigned', What of that I trow?
Some men by feigning words as dark as mine,

. its rays to shine.
' Speak man thy mind.
metaphors make us

: the pen
 divine to men:
dness, because
 not God's laws,
ime held forth

Come, let my carper to his life now look,
And find there darker lines than in my book
He findeth any. Yea, and let him know
That in his best things there are worse lines too.
　May we but stand before impartial men,
To his poor one, I durst adventure ten
That they will take my meaning in these lines
Far better than his lies in silver shrines.
Come, truth, although in swaddling-clouts, I find
Informs the judgement, rectifies the mind,
Pleases the understanding, makes the will
Submit; the memory too it doth fill
With what doth our imagination please,
Likewise, it tends our troubles to appease.
　Sound words I know Timothy is to use,[5]
And old wives' fables he is to refuse,
But yet grave Paul him nowhere doth forbid
The use of parables; in which lay hid
That gold, those pearls, and precious stones that
　　were
Worth digging for, and that with greatest care.
　Let me add one word more, O man of God!
Art thou offended? Dost thou wish I had
Put forth my matter in another dress,
Or that I had in things been more express?
Three things let me propound, then I submit
To those that are my betters (as is fit).
　1. I find not that I am denied the use
Of this my method, so I no abuse
Put on the words, things, readers, or be rude
In handling figure, or similitude,
In application; but all that I may
Seek the advance of Truth this or that way.
Denied did I say? Nay, I have leave
(Example too, and that from them that have
God better pleased by their words or ways

breatheth nowadays),
mind, thus to declare
at excellentest are.
(as high as trees) will write
t no man doth them slight
ed if they abuse
y, and the craft they use
yet let truth be free
upon thee, and me,
s God. For who knows how,
taught us first to plough,
and pens for his design?
things usher in divine.
y Writ in many places
h this method, where the cases
ing to set forth another:
and yet nothing smother
ns, nay, by this method may
s rays as light as day.
I do put up my pen,
of my book, and then
and it unto that hand
g down, and makes weak ones

keth out before thine eyes
the everlasting prize:
ce he comes, whither he goes,
lone, also what he does:
ow he runs, and runs,
te of Glory comes.
sets out for life amain,
wn they would attain:
see the reason why
ur, and like fools do die.
ake a traveller of thee,
ou wilt ruled be;

It will direct thee to the Holy Land,
If thou wilt its directions understand:
Yea, it will make the slothful active be,
The blind also delightful things to see.
   Art thou for something rare, and profitable?
Would'st thou see a truth within a fable?
Art thou forgetful? Wouldest thou remember
From New Year's Day to the last of December?
Then read my fancies, they will stick like burrs,
And may be to the helpless, comforters.
   This book is writ in such a dialect
As may the minds of listless men affect:
It seems a novelty, and yet contains
Nothing but sound and honest gospel-strains.
   Would'st thou divert thyself from melancholy?
Would'st thou be pleasant, yet be far from folly?
Would'st thou read riddles and their explanation,
Or else be drownded in thy contemplation?
Dost thou love picking-meat?[7] Or would'st thou see
A man i' the clouds, and hear him speak to thee?
Would'st thou be in a dream, and yet not sleep?
Or would'st thou in a moment laugh and weep?
Wouldest thou lose thyself, and catch no harm
And find thyself again without a charm?
Would'st read thyself, and read thou know'st not
    what
And yet know whether thou art blest or not,
By reading the same lines? O then come hither,
And lay my book, thy head and heart together.

JOHN BUNYAN

THE PILGRIM'S PROGRESS
in the similitude of a
DREAM

As I walked through the wilderness of this world, I lighted on a certain place, where was a den; *The goal*[8] and I laid me down in that place to sleep: and as I slept I dreamed a dream. I dreamed, and behold I saw a man clothed with rags, standing in a certain place, with his face from his own house, a book in his hand, and a great burden upon his back. I looked, and saw him open the book, and read therein; and as he read, he wept and trembled: and not being able longer to contain, he brake out with a lamentable cry; saying, 'What shall I do?' *His out-cry*

In this plight therefore he went home, and restrained himself as long as he could, that his wife and children should not perceive his distress; but he could not be silent long, because that his trouble increased: wherefore at length he brake his mind to his wife and children; and thus he began to talk to them: 'O my dear wife,' said he, 'and you the children of my bowels, I your dear friend[9] am in myself undone, by reason of a burden that lieth hard upon me: moreover, I am for certain informed that this our city will be burned with fire from Heaven, in which fearful overthrow, both myself, with thee, my wife, and you my sweet babes, shall miserably come to ruin; except (the which yet I see not) some way of escape can be found, whereby we may be delivered.' At this his relations were sore amazed; not for that they believed that what he said to them was true, but because they thought that some frenzy distemper had got into his head: therefore, it drawing towards night, and they hoping that sleep might settle his brains, with all haste they got him to bed; but the night was as troublesome to him as the day: wherefore instead of sleeping, he spent it in sighs and tears. So when the morning was come, they would know how he did and he told them worse and worse. He also set to talking to them again, but they began to be hardened; *Carnal* they also thought to drive away his distemper by *physic for* harsh and surly carriages to him: sometimes they *a sick soul* would deride, sometimes they would chide, and sometimes they would quite neglect him: wherefore he began to retire himself to his chamber to pray for, and pity them; and also to condole his own misery: he would also walk solitarily in the fields,[10] sometimes reading, and sometimes praying: and thus for some days he spent his time.

Now, I saw upon a time, when he was walking in the fields, that he was (as he was wont) reading in his book, and greatly distressed in his mind; and as he read, he burst out, as he had done before, crying, *What shall I do to be saved?*

I saw also that he looked this way, and that way, as if he would run; yet he stood still, because, as I perceived, he could not tell which way to go. I looked then, and saw a man named Evangelist[11] coming to him, and asked, 'Wherefore dost thou cry?' He answered, 'Sir, I perceive, by the book in my hand, that I am condemned to die, and after that to come to judgement; and I find that I am not willing to do the first, nor able to do the second.'

Then said Evangelist, 'Why not willing to die? since this life is attended with so many evils?' The man answered, 'Because I fear that this burden that is upon my back will sink me lower than the grave; and I shall fall into Tophet.[12] And, Sir, if I be not fit to go to prison, I am not fit (I am sure) to go to judgement, and from thence to execution; and the thoughts of these things make me cry.'

Then said Evangelist, 'If this be thy condition, why standest thou still?' He answered, 'Because I know not whither to go.' Then he gave him a parchment roll, and there was written within, *Fly from the wrath to come.*

Conviction of the necessity of flying

The man therefore read it, and looking upon Evangelist very carefully, said, 'Whither must I fly?' Then said Evangelist, pointing with his finger over a very wide field, 'Do you see yonder Wicket Gate?'[13] The man said, 'No.' Then said the other, 'Do you see yonder shining light?' He said, 'I think I do.' Then said Evangelist, 'Keep that light in your eye, and go up directly thereto, so shalt thou see the Gate at which, when thou knockest, it shall be told thee what thou shalt do.'

Christ and the way to him cannot be found without the Word

So I saw in my dream that the man began to run. Now he had not run far from his own door, but his wife and children perceiving it began to cry after him to return: but the man put his fingers in his ears, and ran on crying, 'Life, life, eternal life.' So he looked not behind him, but fled towards the middle of the plain.

The neighbours also came out to see him run, and as he ran some mocked, others threatened; and some cried after him to return. Now among those that did so, there were two that were resolved to fetch him back by force. The name of the one was Obstinate, and the name of the other Pliable. Now by this time the man was got a good distance from them, but however they were resolved to pursue him, which they did and in little time they overtook him. Then said the man, 'Neighbours, wherefore are you come?' They said, 'To persuade you to go back with us.' But he said, 'That can by no means be. You dwell,'

They that fly from the wrath to come, are a gazing-stock to the world

Obstinate and Pliable follow him

said he, 'in the City of Destruction (the place also where I was born), I see it to be so; and dying there, sooner or later, you will sink lower than the grave, into a place that burns with fire and brimstone; be content, good neighbours, and go along with me.'

'What!' said Obstinate, 'and leave our friends and our comforts behind us!'

'Yes,' said Christian (for that was his name), 'because, that all which you shall forsake is not worthy to be compared with a little of that that I am seeking to enjoy, and if you will go along with me, and hold it, you shall fare as I myself; for there where I go is enough and to spare; come away, and prove my words.'

Obstinate. What are the things you seek, since you leave all the world to find them?

Christian. I seek an inheritance, incorruptible, undefiled, and that fadeth not away; and it is laid up in Heaven, and fast there, to be bestowed at the time appointed, on them that diligently seek it. Read it so, if you will, in my book.

Obstinate. Tush, said Obstinate, away with your book; will you go back with us, or no?

Christian. No, not I, said the other; because I have laid my hand to the plough.

Obstinate. Come then, neighbour Pliable, let us turn again, and go home without him; there is a company of these crazed-headed coxcombs that when they take a fancy by the end are wiser in their own eyes than seven men that can render a reason.

Pliable. Then said Pliable, Don't revile; if what the good Christian says is true, the things he looks after are better than ours; my heart inclines to go with my neighbour.

Obstinate. What! more fools still? Be ruled by me and go back. Who knows whither such a brain-sick fellow will lead you? Go back, go back, and be wise.

Christian. Come with me neighbour Pliable, there are such things to be had which I spoke of, and many more glories besides. If you believe not me, read here in this book; and for the truth of what is expressed therein, behold, all is confirmed by the blood of him that made it.

Pliable. Well neighbour Obstinate (said Pliable) I begin to come to a point; I intend to go along with this good man, and to cast in my lot with him. But my good companion, do you know the way to this desired place?

Christian. I am directed by a man whose name is Evangelist, to speed me to a little Gate that is before us, where we shall receive instruction about the way.

Pliable. Come then, good neighbour, let us be going. Then they went both together.

Obstinate. And I will go back to my place, said Obstinate; I will be no companion of such misled fantastical fellows.

Now I saw in my dream, that when Obstinate was gone back, Christian and Pliable went talking over the plain; and thus they began their discourse:

Christian. Come neighbour Pliable, how do you do? I am glad you are persuaded to go along with me, and had even Obstinate himself but felt what I have felt of the powers and terrors of what is yet unseen, he would not thus lightly have given us the back.

Pliable. Come neighbour Christian, since there is none but us two here, tell me now further, what the things are, and how to be enjoyed, whither we are going.

Christian. I can better conceive of them with my mind, than speak of them with my tongue; but yet

Christian and Obstinate pull for Pliable's soul

Pliable consented to go with Christian

Talk between Christian and Pliable

us to know, I will read of them

ou think that the words of your rue?

ily, for it was made by him that

what things are they?

is an endless Kingdom to be asting life to be given us; that we ngdom for ever.

and what else?

are crowns of glory to be given at will make us shine like the sun heaven.

cellent; and what else?

shall be no more crying, nor s owner of the place will wipe all

company shall we have there? we shall be with Seraphims, and s that will dazzle your eyes to here also you shall meet with housands that have gone before e of them are hurtful, but loving, walking in the sight of God and sence with acceptance for ever: e shall see the elders with their re we shall see the holy virgins arps. There we shall see men that ut in pieces, burnt in flames, eaten

Christian. The Lord, the governor of that country, hath recorded that in this book, the substance of which is, if we be truly willing to have it, he will bestow it upon us freely.

Pliable. Well, my good companion, glad am I to hear of these things: come on, let us mend our pace.

Christian. I cannot go so fast as I would, by reason of this burden that is upon my back.

Now I saw in my dream, that just as they had ended this talk, they drew near to a very miry Slough that was in the midst of the plain, and they, being heedless, did both fall suddenly into the bog. The name of the Slough was Despond.[14] Here therefore they wallowed for a time, being grievously bedaubed with the dirt, and Christian, because of the burden that was on his back, began to sink in the mire.

Pliable. Then said Pliable, Ah, neighbour Christian, where are you now?

Christian. Truly, said Christian, I do not know.

Pliable. At that Pliable began to be offended, and angerly, said to his fellow, Is this the happiness you have told me all this while of? If we have such ill speed at our first setting out, what may we expect, 'twixt this and our journey's end? May I get out again with my life you shall possess the brave country alone for me. And with that he gave a desperate struggle or two, and got out of the mire on that side of the Slough which was next to his own house. So away he went, and Christian saw him no more.

It is not enough to be pliable

Wherefore Christian was left to tumble in the Slough of Despond alone; but still he endeavoured to struggle to that side of the Slough that was still further from his own house, and next to the Wicket Gate; the which he did, but could not get out,

Christian in trouble, seeks still to get further from his own house

en that was upon his back; but
1, that a man came to him, whose
asked him what he did there.

Christian, I was bid go this way,
ngelist, who directed me also to
might escape the wrath to come;
hither, I fell in here.

d you not look for the steps?
lowed me so hard, that I fled the

ie, Give me thy hand; so he gave
he drew him out, and set him
, and bid him go on his way.

him that plucked him out, and
, since over this place is the way
estruction, to yonder Gate, is it,
ot mended, that poor travellers
ith more security?' And he said
Slough is such a place as cannot
e descent whither the scum and
nviction for sin doth continually
it called the Slough of Despond:
ner is awakened about his lost
seth in his soul many fears, and
aging apprehensions, which all of
nd settle in this place; and this is
dness of this ground.

isure of the King that this place
d; his labourers also, have, by the
jesty's surveyors, been for above
d years,[16] employed about this
if perhaps it might have been

that have at all seasons been brought from all places of the King's dominions (and they that can tell, say they are the best materials to make good ground of the place); if so be it might have been mended, but it is the Slough of Despond still, and so will be when they have done what they can.

'True, there are by the direction of the law-giver, certain good and substantial steps, placed even through the very midst of this Slough; but at such time as this place doth much spew out its filth, as it doth against change of weather, these steps are hardly seen; or if they be, men through the dizziness of their heads step besides; and then they are bemired to purpose, notwithstanding the steps be there; but the ground is good when they are once got in at the Gate.' *The promises of forgiveness and acceptance to life by faith in Christ*

Now I saw in my dream, that by this time Pliable was got home to his house again. So his neighbours came to visit him; and some of them called him wise man for coming back; and some called him fool for hazarding himself with Christian; others again did mock at his cowardliness, saying, 'Surely since you began to venture, I would not have been so base to have given out for a few difficulties.' So Pliable sat sneaking among them. But at last he got more confidence, and then they all turned their tales, and began to deride poor Christian behind his back. And thus much concerning Pliable. *Pliable got home, and is visited of his neighbours. His entertainment by them at his return*

Now as Christian was walking solitary by himself, he espied one afar off come crossing over the field to meet him; and their hap was to meet just as they were crossing the way of each other. The gentleman's name was Mr Worldly-Wiseman,[17] he dwelt in the town of Carnal-Policy, a very great town, and also hard by from whence Christian came. This man then meeting with Christian, and having some inkling of *Mr Worldly-Wiseman meets with Christian*

setting forth from the City of
noised abroad, not only in the
lt, but also it began to be the
other places, Master Worldly-
having some guess of him, by
rious going, by observing his
the like, began thus to enter into
stian.

How now, good fellow, whither
ened manner?

ened manner indeed, as ever I
had. And whereas you ask me,
ll you, sir, I am going to yonder
me; for there, as I am informed,
a way to be rid of my heavy

Christian. A man that appeared to me to be a very great and honourable person; his name, as I remember, is Evangelist.

Worldly-Wiseman. I beshrew him for his counsel; there is not a more dangerous and troublesome way in the world than is that unto which he hath directed thee, and that thou shalt find if thou wilt be ruled by his counsel. Thou hast met with something (as I perceive) already; for I see the dirt of the Slough of Despond is upon thee; but that Slough is the beginning of the sorrows that do attend those that go on in that way; hear me, I am older than thou! Thou art like to meet with in the way which thou goest, wearisomeness, painfulness, hunger, perils, nakedness, sword, lions, dragons, darkness, and in a word, death, and what not? These things are certainly true, having been confirmed by many testimonies. And why should a man so carelessly cast away himself by giving heed to a stranger. *Mr Worldly-Wiseman condemned Evangelist's counsel*

Christian. Why, sir, this burden upon my back is more terrible to me than are all these things which you have mentioned: nay, methinks I care not what I meet with in the way, so be I can also meet with deliverance from my burden. *The frame of the heart of young Christians*

Worldly-Wiseman. How camest thou by thy burden at first?

Christian. By reading this book in my hand.

Worldly-Wiseman. I thought so; and it is happened unto thee as to other weak men, who meddling with things too high for them, do suddenly fall into thy distractions; which distractions do not only unman men (as thine I perceive has done thee), but they run them upon desperate ventures, to obtain they know not what. *Worldly-Wiseman does not like that men should be serious in reading the Bible*

Christian. I know what I would obtain; it is ease for my heavy burden.

to: yea, and the remedy is at
add, that instead of those dangers,
th much safety, friendship, and

r, open this secret to me.

Why, in yonder village (the
orality) there dwells a gentleman,
ality, a very judicious man (and
ood name) that has skill to help
burdens as thine are, from their
my knowledge he hath done a
this way: ay, and besides, he hath
nat are somewhat crazed in their
rdens. To him, as I said, thou
elped presently. His house is not
his place; and if he should not be
hath a pretty young man to his
Civility, that can do it (to speak on)
gentleman himself. There, I say,
d of thy burden, and if thou art
ack to thy former habitation, as
wish thee, thou mayest send for
en to thee to this village, where
ow stand empty, one of which
at reasonable rates; provision is
good, and that which will make
happy, is, to be sure there thou
neighbours, in credit and good

tian somewhat at a stand, but
ded; if this be true which this

gentleman hath said, my wisest course is to take his advice, and with that he thus further spoke.

Christian. Sir, which is my way to this honest man's house?

Worldly-Wiseman. Do you see yonder high Hill?[18]   *Mount Sinai*

Christian. Yes, very well.

Worldly-Wiseman. By that Hill you must go, and the first house you come at is his.

So Christian turned out of his way to go to Mr Legality's house for help: but behold, when he was got now hard by the Hill, it seemed so high, and also that side of it that was next the way side, did hang so much over, that Christian was afraid to venture *Christian* further, lest the Hill should fall on his head: where- *afraid that* fore there he stood still, and wotted not what to do. *Mount Sinai* Also his burden, now, seemed heavier to him, than *would fall on* while he was in his way. There came also flashes of *his head* fire out of the Hill, that made Christian afraid that he should be burned: here therefore he sweat, and did quake for fear. And now he began to be sorry that he had taken Mr Worldly-Wiseman's counsel; and with that he saw Evangelist coming to meet him; at *Evangelist* the sight also of whom he began to blush for shame. *findeth* So Evangelist drew nearer, and nearer, and coming *Christian* up to him, he looked upon him with a severe and *under Mount* dreadful countenance, and thus began to reason with *Sinai and* Christian. *looketh severely upon him*

Evangelist. What doest thou here? said he; at which *Evangelist* word Christian knew not what to answer: where- *reasons afresh* fore, at present he stood speechless before him. Then *with Christian* said Evangelist further, Art not thou the man that I found crying, without the walls of the City of Destruction?

Christian. Yes, dear sir, I am the man.

Evangelist. Did not I direct thee the way to the little Wicket Gate?

Christian. Yes, dear sir, said Christian.

Evangelist. How is it then that thou art so quickly turned aside, for thou art now out of the way?

Christian. I met with a gentleman, so soon as I had got over the Slough of Despond, who persuaded me that I might in the village before me find a man that could take off my burden.

Evangelist. What was he?

Christian. He looked like a gentleman, and talked much to me, and got me at last to yield; so I came hither: but when I beheld this Hill, and how it hangs over the way, I suddenly made a stand, lest it should fall on my head.

Evangelist. What said that gentleman to you?

Christian. Why, he asked me whither I was going, and I told him.

Evangelist. And what said he then?

Christian. He asked me if I had a family, and I told him: but, said I, I am so loaden with the burden that is on my back that I cannot take pleasure in them as formerly.

Evangelist. And what said he then?

Christian. He bid me with speed get rid of my burden and I told him 'twas ease that I sought; and, said I, I am therefore going to yonder Gate to receive further direction how I may get to the place of deliverance. So he said that he would show me a better way, and short, not so attended with difficulties as the way, sir, that you set me; 'which way,' said he, 'will direct you to a gentleman's house that hath skill to take off these burdens.' So I believed him, and turned out of that way into this, if haply I might be soon eased of my burden: but when I came to this place, and beheld things as they are, I stopped for fear (as I said) of danger: but I now know not what to do.

Evangelist. Then (said Evangelist) stand still a little, that I may show thee the words of God. So he stood trembling. Then (said Evangelist) See that ye refuse not him that speaketh; for if they escaped not who refused him that spake on earth, much more shall not we escape, if we turn away from him that speaketh from Heaven. He said moreover, *Now the just shall live by faith; but if any man draw back, my soul shall have no pleasure in him.*[19] He also did thus apply them, Thou art the man that art running into this misery, thou hast began to reject the counsel of the most high, and to draw back thy foot from the way of peace, even almost to the hazarding of thy perdition.

Evangelist convinces Christian of his error

Then Christian fell down at his foot as dead, crying, 'Woe is me, for I am undone', at the sight of which Evangelist caught him by the right hand, saying, 'All manner of sin and blasphemies shall be forgiven unto men; be not faithless, but believing.' Then did Christian again a little revive, and stood up trembling, as at first, before Evangelist.

Then Evangelist proceeded, saying, 'Give more earnest heed to the things that I shall tell thee of. I will now show thee who it was that deluded thee, and who 'twas also to whom he sent thee. The man that met thee is one Worldly-Wiseman, and rightly is he so called; partly, because he favoureth only the doctrine of this world (therefore he always goes to the town of Morality to church) and partly because he loveth that doctrine best, for it saveth him from the Cross; and because he is of this carnal temper, therefore he seeketh to prevent my ways, though right. Now there are three things in this man's counsel that thou must utterly abhor.

Mr Worldly-Wiseman described by Evangelist

Evangelist discovers the deceit of Mr Worldly-Wiseman

1. His turning thee out of the way.
2. His labouring to render the Cross odious to thee.

3. And his setting thy feet in that way that leadeth unto the administration of death.

'First, thou must abhor his turning thee out of the way; yea, and thine own consenting thereto: because this is to reject the counsel of God, for the sake of the counsel of a Worldly-Wiseman. The Lord says, *Strive to enter in at the strait gate*, the Gate to which I sent thee; *for strait is the gate that leadeth unto life, and few there be that find it*. From this little Wicket Gate, and from the way thereto hath this wicked man turned thee, to the bringing of thee almost to destruction; hate therefore his turning thee out of the way, and abhor thyself for hearkening to him.

'Secondly, thou must abhor his labouring to render the Cross odious unto thee; for thou art to prefer it before the treasures in Egypt: besides the King of Glory hath told thee, that he that will save his life shall lose it: and *he that comes after him, and hates not his father and mother, and wife, and children, and brethren, and sisters; yea, and his own life also, he cannot be my disciple.* I say therefore, for a man to labour to persuade thee, that that shall be thy death, without which the truth hath said, thou canst not have eternal life, this doctrine thou must abhor.

'Thirdly, thou must hate his setting of thy feet in the way that leadeth to the ministration of death. And for this thou must consider to whom he sent thee, and also how unable that person was to deliver thee from thy burden.

'He to whom thou wast sent for ease, being by name Legality, is the son of the bond-woman which now is, and is in bondage with her children, and is in *The bond-woman* a mystery this Mount Sinai, which thou hast feared will fall on thy head. Now if she with her children are in bondage, how canst thou expect by them to be made free? This Legality therefore is not able to set

66

thee free from thy burden. No man was as yet ever rid of his burden by him, no, nor ever is like to be: ye cannot be justified by the works of the law; for by the deeds of the law no man living can be rid of his burden: therefore Mr Worldly-Wiseman is an alien, and Mr Legality a cheat, and for his son Civility, notwithstanding his simpering looks, he is but an hypocrite, and cannot help thee. Believe me, there is nothing in all this noise that thou hast heard of this sottish man, but a design to beguile thee of thy salvation, by turning thee from the way in which I had set thee.' After this Evangelist called aloud to the Heavens for confirmation of what he had said; and with that there came words and fire out of the mountain under which poor Christian stood, that made the hair of his flesh stand. The words were thus pronounced, *As many as are of the works of the law, are under the curse; for it is written, Cursed is every one that continueth not in all things which are written in the book of the law to do them.*

Now Christian looked for nothing but death, and began to cry out lamentably, even cursing the time in which he met with Mr Worldly-Wiseman, still calling himself a thousand fools for hearkening to his counsel: he also was greatly ashamed to think that this gentleman's arguments, flowing only from the flesh, should have that prevalency with him as to cause him to forsake the right way. This done, he applied himself again to Evangelist in words and sense as follows.

Christian. Sir, what think you? Is there hopes? May I now go back and go up to the Wicket Gate, shall I not be abandoned for this, and sent back from thence ashamed. I am sorry I have hearkened to this man's counsel, but may my sin be forgiven. *Christian inquired if he may yet be happy*

Evangelist. Then said Evangelist to him, Thy sin is

very great, for by it thou hast committed two evils; thou hast forsaken the way that is good, to tread in *Evangelist* forbidden paths: yet will the man at the Gate receive *comforts him* thee, for he has good will for men; only, said he, take heed that thou turn not aside again, lest thou perish from the way when his wrath is kindled but a little. Then did Christian address himself to go back, and Evangelist, after he had kissed him, gave him one smile, and bid him godspeed; so he went on with haste, neither spake he to any man by the way; nor if any man asked him, would he vouchsafe them an answer. He went like one that was all the while treading on forbidden ground, and could by no means think himself safe, till again he was got into the way which he left to follow Mr Worldly-Wiseman's counsel: so in process of time Christian got up to the Gate. Now over the Gate there was written, *Knock and it shall be opened unto you.* He knocked therefore, more than once or twice, saying,

> *May I now enter here? Will he within*
> *Open to sorry me, though I have been*
> *An undeserving rebel? Then shall I,*
> *Not fail to sing his lasting praise on high.*

At last there came a grave person to the Gate named Good Will, who asked who was there, and whence he came, and what he would have.

Christian. Here is a poor burdened sinner, I come from the City of Destruction, but am going to Mount Sion, that I may be delivered from the wrath to come; I would therefore, sir, since I am informed that by this Gate is the way thither, know if you are *The gate* willing to let me in.

will be *Good Will.* I am willing with all my heart, said he; *opened to* and with that he opened the Gate.[20] *broken-hearted* *sinners* So when Christian was stepping in, the other gave him a pull: Then said Christian, 'What means that?' The other told him, 'A little distance from this Gate, there is erected a strong castle, of which Beelzebub[21] is the captain: from thence both he, and them that are with him, shoot arrows at those that come up to this Gate, if happily they may die before they can enter in.' Then,' said Christian, 'I rejoice and tremble.' So when he was got in, the man of the Gate asked him who directed him thither.

Christian. Evangelist bid me come hither and knock (as I did). And he said that you, sir, would tell me what I must do.

Good Will. An open door is set before thee, and no man can shut it.

Christian. Now I begin to reap the benefits of my hazards.

Good Will. But how is it that you came alone?

Christian. Because none of my neighbours saw their danger as I saw mine.

Good Will. Did any of them know of your coming?

Christian. Yes, my wife and children saw me at the first, and called after me to turn again. Also some of my neighbours stood crying, and calling after me to return; but I put my fingers in mine ears, and so came on my way.

Good Will. But did none of them follow you to persuade you to go back?

Christian. Yes, both Obstinate and Pliable; but when they saw that they could not prevail, Obstinate went railing back, but Pliable came with me a little way.

Good Will. But why did he not come through?

Christian. We indeed came both together, until we came at the Slough of Despond, into the which we also suddenly fell. And then was my neighbour Pliable discouraged, and would not adventure fur-

Satan envies those that enter the Strait Gate

Christian entered the Gate with joy and trembling

Talk between Good Will and Christian

A man may have company when he sets out for Heaven, and yet go thither alone ther. Wherefore getting out again, on that side next to his own house, he told me I should possess the brave country alone for him; so he went his way, and I came mine. He after Obstinate, and I to this Gate.

Good Will. Then said Good Will, Alas, poor man, is the celestial glory of so small esteem with him that he counteth it not worth running the hazards of a few difficulties to obtain it?

Christian. Truly, said Christian, I have said the truth of Pliable, and if I should also say all the truth *Christian* of myself, it will appear there is no betterment 'twixt *accuseth* him and myself. 'Tis true, he went back to his own *himself* house, but I also turned aside to go in the way of *before the* death, being persuaded thereto by the carnal argu- *man at the* ments of one Mr Worldly-Wiseman. *gate*

Good Will. Oh, did he light upon you! What, he would have had you a sought for[22] ease at the hands of Mr Legality; they are both of them a very cheat: but did you take his counsel?

Christian. Yes, as far as I durst, I went to find out Mr Legality, until I thought that the Mountain that stands by his house would have fallen upon my head: wherefore there I was forced to stop.

Good Will. That Mountain has been the death of many, and will be the death of many more: 'tis well you escaped being by it dashed in pieces.

Christian. Why, truly I do not know what had become of me there, had not Evangelist happily met me again as I was musing in the midst of my dumps: but 'twas God's mercy that he came to me again, for else I had never come hither. But now I am come, such a one as I am, more fit indeed for death by that Mountain, than thus to stand talking with my Lord. But oh, what a favour is this to me, that yet I am *Christian is* admitted entrance here. *comforted* *again* *Good Will.* We make no objections against any, notwithstanding all that they have done before they come hither, they in no wise are cast out; and therefore, good Christian, come a little way with me, and I will teach thee about the way thou must go. Look before thee; dost thou see this narrow way? That is the way thou must go. It was cast up by the patriarchs, prophets, Christ, and his apostles, and it is as straight as a rule can make it. This is the way thou must go. *Christian directed yet on his way*

Christian. But said Christian, Is there no turnings nor windings, by which a stranger may lose the way? *Christian afraid of losing his way*

Good Will. Yes, there are many ways butt down upon[23] this; and they are crooked, and wide; but thus thou may'st distinguish the right from the wrong, that only being straight and narrow.

Then I saw in my dream that Christian asked him further if he could not help him off with his burden that was upon his back; for as yet he had not got rid thereof, nor could he by any means get it off without help. *Christian weary of his burden*

He told him, 'As to the burden, be content to bear it, until thou comest to the place of deliverance; for there it will fall from thy back itself.' *There is no deliverance from the guilt and burden of sin, but by the death and blood of Christ*

Then Christian began to gird up his loins, and to address himself to his journey. So the other told him that by that he was gone some distance from the Gate he would come at the House of the Interpreter,[4] at whose door he should knock; and he would show him excellent things. Then Christian took his leave of his friend, and he again bid him godspeed.

Then he went on, till he came at the House of the Interpreter,[24] where he knocked, over and over; at last one came to the door, and asked who was there. *Christian comes to the House of the Interpreter*

Christian. Sir, here is a traveller, who was bid by an acquaintance of the good man of this House, to call here for my profit: I would therefore speak with the master of the House. So he called for the master of the House, who after a little time came to Christian and asked him what he would have.

Christian. Sir, said Christian, I am a man that am come from the City of Destruction, and am going to the Mount Sion, and I was told by the man that stands at the Gate, at the head of this way that if I called here, you would show me excellent things, such as would be an help to me in my journey.

He is entertained *Interpreter.* Then said the Interpreter, Come in, I will show thee that which will be profitable to thee.

Illumination So he commanded his man to light the candle, and bid Christian follow him; so he had him into a private room, and bid his man open a door, the which *Christian sees a brave picture* when he had done, Christian saw a picture of a very grave person[25] hang up against the wall, and this was *The fashion of the picture* the fashion of it: it had eyes lift up to Heaven, the best of books in its hand, the law of truth was written upon its lips, the world was behind its back; it stood as if it pleaded with men, and a crown of gold did hang over its head.

Christian. Then said Christian, What means this?

Interpreter. The man whose picture this is is one of a thousand; he can beget children, travail in birth with children, and nurse them himself when they are born. And whereas thou seest him with his eyes lift up to Heaven, the best of books in his hand, and the law of truth writ on his lips, it is to show thee that his work is to know, and unfold dark things to *The meaning of the picture* sinners even as also thou seest him stand as if he pleaded with men; and whereas thou seest the world as cast behind him, and that a crown hangs over his head, that is to show thee that slighting and despising the things that are present, for the love that he hath to his Master's service, he is sure in the world that comes next to have glory for his reward. Now, said the Interpreter, I have showed thee this picture first, because the man whose picture this is, is the only *Why he* man whom the Lord of the Place whither thou art *showed him* going hath authorized to be thy guide in all difficult *first* places thou mayest meet with in the way; wherefore take good heed to what I have showed thee, and bear well in thy mind what thou hast seen, lest in thy journey thou meet with some that pretend to lead thee right, but their way goes down to death.

Then he took him by the hand, and led him into a very large parlour that was full of dust, because never swept; the which, after he had reviewed a little while, the Interpreter called for a man to sweep: now when he began to sweep, the dust began so abundantly to fly about, that Christian had almost therewith been choked. Then said the Interpreter to a damsel that stood by, 'Bring hither water, and sprinkle the room', which when she had done, was swept and cleansed with pleasure.

Christian. Then said Christian, What means this?

Interpreter. The Interpreter answered: This parlour is the heart of a man that was never sanctified by the sweet grace of the Gospel; that dust is his original sin, and inward corruptions that have defiled the whole man. He that began to sweep at first is the Law, but she that brought water, and did sprinkle it, is the Gospel. Now, whereas thou sawest that so soon as the first began to sweep, the dust did so fly about that the room by him could not be cleansed, but that thou wast almost choked therewith, this is to show thee that the Law, instead of cleansing the heart (by its working) from sin, doth revive, put strength into, and increase it in the soul, even as it doth discover and forbid it, for it doth not give power to subdue.

Again, as thou sawest the damsel sprinkle the room

with water, upon which it was cleansed with pleasure: this is to show thee that when the Gospel comes in the sweet and precious influences thereof to the heart, then I say, even as thou sawest the damsel lay the dust by sprinkling the floor with water, so is sin vanquished and subdued, and the soul made clean, through the faith of it; and consequently fit for the King of Glory to inhabit.

He showed him Passion and Patience. Passion will have all now I saw moreover in my dream, that the Interpreter took him by the hand, and had him into a little room, where sat two little children, each one in his chair: the name of the eldest was Passion, and of the other, Patience; Passion seemed to be much discontent, but Patience was very quiet. Then Christian asked, 'What is the reason of the discontent of Passion?' The Interpreter answered, 'The Governor of them would have him stay for his best things till the beginning of the next year, but he will have all now: *Patience is for waiting, Passion has his desire* but Patience is willing to wait.'

Then I saw that one came to Passion, and brought him a bag of treasure, and poured it down at his feet; the which he took up, and rejoiced therein, and withal, laughed Patience to scorn. But I beheld but *And quickly lavishes all away* a while, and he had lavished all away, and had nothing left him but rags.

The matter expounded *Christian.* Then said Christian to the Interpreter, Expound this matter more fully to me.

Interpreter. So he said, These two lads are figures, Passion, of the men of this world, and Patience, of the men of that which is to come; for as here thou seest, Passion will have all now, this year; that is to say, in this world; so are the men of this world: they must have all their good things now, they cannot *The worldly man for a bird in the hand* stay till next year; that is, until the next world, for their portion of good. That proverb, 'A bird in the hand is worth two in the bush', is of more authority with them, than are all the divine testimonies of the good of the world to come. But as thou sawest, that he had quickly lavished all away, and had presently left him nothing but rags; so will it be with all such men at the end of this world.

Christian. Then said Christian, Now I see that Patience has the best wisdom, and that upon many accounts. 1. Because he stays for the best things. 2. And also because he will have the glory of his, when the other hath nothing but rags.

Patience had the best wisdom

Interpreter. Nay, you may add another; to wit, the glory of the next world will never wear out; but these are suddenly gone. Therefore Passion had not so much reason to laugh at Patience because he had his good things first, as Patience will have to laugh at Passion because he had his best things last; for first must give place to last, because last must have his time to come, but last gives place to nothing, for there is not another to succeed; he therefore that hath his portion first, must needs have a time to spend it, but he that has his portion last must have it lastingly. Therefore it is said of Dives, *In thy life thou received'st thy good things, and likewise Lazarus evil things; but now he is comforted, and thou art tormented.*[26]

Things that are first must give place, but things that are last are lasting

Dives had his good things first

Christian. Then I perceive, 'tis not best to covet things that are now, but to wait for things to come.

Interpreter. You say the truth, *For the things that are seen, are temporal; but the things that are not seen, are eternal.* But though this be so, yet since things present and our fleshly appetite are such near neighbours one to another, and again, because things to come, and carnal sense, are such strangers one to another, therefore it is that the first of these so suddenly fall into amity, and that distance is so continued between the second.

The first things are but temporal

Then I saw in my dream that the Interpreter took

and, and led him into a place
urning against a wall, and one
s, casting much water upon it to
ie fire burn higher and hotter.
in, 'What means this?'
iswered, 'This fire is the work of
;ht in the heart; he that casts water
ish and put it out, is the Devil:
t the fire, notwithstanding, burn
thou shalt also see the reason of
about to the backside of the wall,
n with a vessel of oil in his hand,
also continually cast, but secretly,
aid Christian, 'What means this?'
wered, 'This is Christ, who con-
l of his grace maintains the work
e heart, by the means of which,
iat the Devil can do, the souls of
icious still. And in that thou saw-
)od behind the wall to maintain
each thee that it is hard for the
this work of grace is maintained

ie Interpreter took him again by
m into a pleasant place where was
.lace, beautiful to behold; at the
ristian was greatly delighted; he
)p thereof certain persons walked
all in gold. Then said Christian,
ther?' Then the Interpreter took
p toward the door of the palace;
door stood a great company of
go in, but durst not. There also
le distance from the door, at a
ook, and his inkhorn before him,
f him that should enter therein.

He saw also that in the doorway stood many men in armour to keep it, being resolved to do to the man that would enter what hurt and mischief they could. Now was Christian somewhat in a muse; at last, when every man started back for fear of the armed men, Christian saw a man of a very stout countenance[28] come up to the man that sat there to write, saying, 'Set down my name, Sir,' the which when he had done, he saw the man draw his sword, and put an helmet upon his head, and rush toward the door upon the armed men, who laid upon him with deadly force; but the man, not at all discouraged, fell to cutting and hacking most fiercely; so after he had received and given many wounds to those that attempted to keep him out, he cut his way through them all, and pressed forward into the palace; at which there was a pleasant voice heard from those that were within, even of the three[29] that walked upon the top of the palace, saying,

The valiant man

> *Come in, come in;*
> *Eternal Glory thou shalt win.*

So he went in, and was clothed with such garments as they. Then Christian smiled, and said, 'I think verily I know the meaning of this'.

'Now,' said Christian, 'let me go hence.' 'Nay, stay,' said the Interpreter, 'till I have showed thee a little more, and after that, thou shalt go on thy way.' So he took him by the hand again, and led him into a very dark room, where there sat a man in an iron cage.

Despair like an iron cage

Now the man, to look on, seemed very sad: he sat with his eyes looking down to the ground, his hands folded together, and he sighed as if he would break his heart. Then said Christian, 'What means this?' At which the Interpreter bid him talk with the man.

id Christian to the man, What
answered, 'I am what I was not

ast thou once?
d. I was once a fair and flourish-

threatenings, fearful threatenings of certain judgement and fiery indignation, which shall devour me as an adversary.

Christian. For what did you bring yourself into this condition?

Man. For the lusts, pleasures, and profits of this world; in the enjoyment of which I did then promise myself much delight: but now even every one of those things also bite me and gnaw me like a burning worm.

Christian. But canst thou not now repent and turn?

Man. God hath denied me repentance; his word gives me no encouragement to believe; yea, himself hath shut me up in this iron cage: nor can all the men in the world let me out. O eternity! eternity! how shall I grapple with the misery that I must meet with in eternity?

Interpreter. Then said the Interpreter to Christian, Let this man's misery be remembered by thee, and be an everlasting caution to thee.

Christian. Well, said Christian, this is fearful; God help me to watch and be sober; and to pray, that I may shun the cause of this man's misery. Sir, is it not time for me to go on my way now?

Interpreter. Tarry till I shall show thee one thing more, and then thou shalt go on thy way.

So he took Christian by the hand again, and led him into a chamber, where there was one a rising out of bed; and as he put on his raiment he shook and trembled. Then said Christian, 'Why doth this man thus tremble?' The Interpreter then bid him tell to Christian the reason of his so doing: so he began, and said, 'This night as I was in my sleep, I dreamed, and behold the heavens grew exceeding black; also it thundered and lightened in most fearful wise, that it put me into an agony. So I looked up in my dream, and saw the clouds rack* at an unusual rate, upon which I heard a great sound of a trumpet, and saw also a man sit upon a cloud, attended with the thousands of Heaven; they were all in flaming fire, also the heavens was on a burning flame. I heard then a voice, saying, 'Arise ye dead, and come to judgement,' and with that the rocks rent, the graves opened, and the dead that were therein came forth; some of them were exceeding glad, and looked upward, and some sought to hide themselves under the mountains. Then I saw the man that sat upon the cloud open the book and bid the world draw near. Yet there was by reason of a fiery flame that issued out and came from before him a convenient distance betwixt him and them, as betwixt the judge and the prisoners at the bar. I heard it also proclaimed to them that attended on the man that sat on the cloud, 'Gather together the tares, the chaff, and stubble, and cast them into the burning lake,' and with that the bottomless pit opened, just whereabout I stood; out of the mouth of which there came in an abundant manner smoke, and coals of fire, with hideous noises. It was also said to the same persons 'Gather my wheat into my garner.' And with that I saw many catched up and carried away into the clouds, but I was left behind. I also sought to hide myself, but I could not; for the man that sat upon the cloud still kept his eye upon me: my sins also came into mind, and my conscience did accuse me on every side. Upon this I awaked from my sleep.

Christian. But what was it that made you so afraid of this sight?

Man. Why, I thought that the Day of Judgement

* Move.

was come, and that I was not ready for it: but this frighted me most, that the angels gathered up several, and left me behind; also the pit of Hell opened her mouth just where I stood; my conscience too within afflicted me; and as I thought, the Judge had always his eye upon me, showing indignation in his countenance.

Then said the Interpreter to Christian, 'Hast thou considered all these things?'

Christian. Yes, and they put me in hope and fear.

Interpreter. Well, keep all things so in thy mind, that they may be as a goad in thy sides, to prick thee forward in the way thou must go. Then Christian began to gird up his loins, and to address himself to his journey. Then said the Interpreter, The Comforter be always with thee good Christian, to guide thee in the way that leads to the City.

So Christian went on his way, saying,

Here I have seen things rare, and profitable;
Things pleasant, dreadful, things to make me stable
In what I have begun to take in hand:
Then let me think on them, and understand
Wherefore they showed me was, and let me be
Thankful, O good Interpreter, to thee.

Now I saw in my dream, that the highway up which Christian was to go, was fenced on either side with a Wall, and that Wall is called Salvation. Up this way therefore did burdened Christian run, but not without great difficulty, because of the load on his back.

He ran thus till he came at a place somewhat ascending; and upon that place stood a Cross,[33] and a little below in the bottom, a sepulchre. So I saw in my dream, that just as Christian came up with the Cross, his burden loosed from off his shoulders, and fell from off his back; and began to tumble, and so continued to do till it came to the mouth of the sepulchre, where it fell in, and I saw it no more.

When God releases us of our guilt and burden, we are as those that leap for joy

Then was Christian glad and lightsome, and said with a merry heart, 'He hath given me rest, by his sorrow, and life, by his death.' Then he stood still a while, to look and wonder; for it was very surprising to him that the sight of the Cross should thus ease him of his burden. He looked therefore, and looked again, even till the springs that were in his head sent the waters down his cheeks. Now as he stood looking and weeping, behold three Shining Ones[34] came to him, and saluted him, with 'Peace be to thee.' So the first said to him, 'Thy sins be forgiven.' The second stripped him of his rags, and clothed him with change of raiment. The third also set a mark on his forehead, and gave him a roll with a seal upon it, which he bid him look on as he ran, and that he should give it in at the Celestial Gate: so they went their way. Then Christian gave three leaps for joy, and went on singing,

A Christian can sing though alone, when God doth give him the joy of his heart

> Thus far did I come loaden with my sin,
> Nor could aught ease the grief that I was in,
> Till I came hither. What a place is this!
> Must here be the beginning of my bliss?
> Must here the burden fall from off my back?
> Must here the strings that bound it to me, crack?
> Blessed Cross! Blessed Sepulchre! Blessed rather be
> The man that there was put to shame for me.

I saw then in my dream that he went on thus, even until he came at a bottom,[35] where he saw, a little out of the way, three men fast asleep, with fetters upon their heels. The name of the one was Simple, another Sloth, and the third Presumption.

Simple, Sloth, and Presumption

Christian then seeing them lie in this case went to them, if peradventure he might awake them. And cried, 'You are like them that sleep on the top of a mast, for the Dead Sea is under you, a gulf that hath no bottom; awake therefore, and come away; be willing also, and I will help you off with your irons.' He also told them, 'If he that goeth about like a roaring lion comes by, you will certainly become a prey to his teeth.' With that they looked upon him, and began to reply in this sort: Simple said, 'I see no danger'; Sloth said, 'Yet a little more sleep'; and Presumption said, 'Every fat[36] must stand upon his own bottom, what is the answer else that I should give thee?' And so they lay down to sleep again, and Christian went on his way.

There is no persuasion will do, if God openeth not the eyes

Yet was he troubled to think that men in that danger should so little esteem the kindness of him that so freely offered to help them, both by awakening of them, counselling of them, and proffering to help them off with their irons. And as he was troubled thereabout, he espied two men come tumbling over the wall on the left hand of the narrow way; and they made up a pace to him. The name of the one was Formalist, and the name of the other Hypocrisy. So, as I said, they drew up unto him, who thus entered with them into discourse.

Christian. Gentlemen, whence came you, and whither do you go?

Christian talked with them

Formalist and Hypocrisy. We were born in the land of Vainglory, and are going for praise to Mount Sion.

Christian. Why came you not in at the Gate which standeth at the beginning of the way? Know you not that it is written that, *He that cometh not in by the door, but climbeth up some other way, the same is a thief and a robber.*

Formalist and Hypocrisy. They said, that to go to the Gate for entrance, was by all their countrymen counted too far about; and that therefore their usual way was to make a short cut of it, and to climb over the wall as they had done.

Christian. But will it not be counted a trespass against the Lord of the City whither we are bound, thus to violate his revealed will?

They that come into the way, but not by the door, think that they can say something in vindication of their own practice

Formalist and Hypocrisy. They told him, that as for that, he needed not to trouble his head thereabout, for what they did they had custom for; and could produce, if need were, testimony that would witness it for more than a thousand years.

Christian. But said Christian, Will your practice stand a trial at law?

Formalist and Hypocrisy. They told him that custom, it being of so long a standing as above a thousand years,[37] would doubtless now be admitted as a thing legal, by any impartial judge. And besides, said they, so be we get into the way, what's matter which way we get in; if we are in, we are in: thou art but in the way, who, as we perceive, came in at the Gate; and we are also in the way that came tumbling over the wall: wherein now is thy condition better than ours?

Christian. I walk by the rule of my master, you walk by the rude working of your fancies. You are counted thieves already by the Lord of the way, therefore I doubt you will not be found true men at the end of the way. You come in by yourselves without his direction, and shall go out by yourselves without his mercy.

To this they made him but little answer; only they bid him look to himself. Then I saw that they went on every man in his way, without much conference one with another; save that these two men told

84

Christian, that, as to laws and ordinances, they doubted not, but they should as conscientiously do them as he. 'Therefore,' said they, 'we see not wherein thou differest from us, but by the coat that is on thy back,[38] which was, as we trow, given thee by some of thy neighbours to hide the shame of thy nakedness.'

Christian. By laws and ordinances you will not be saved, since you came not in by the door. And as for this coat that is on my back, it was given me by the Lord of the place whither I go; and that, as you say, to cover my nakedness with. And I take it as a token of his kindness to me, for I had nothing but rags before; and besides, thus I comfort myself as I go, surely, think I, when I come to the Gate of the City, the Lord thereof will know me for good, since I have his coat on my back; a coat that he gave me freely in the day that he stripped me of my rags. I have moreover a mark in my forehead, of which perhaps you have taken no notice, which one of my Lord's most intimate associates fixed there in the day that my burden fell off my shoulders. I will tell you moreover, that I had then given me a roll sealed to comfort me by reading, as I go in the way; I was also bid to give it in at the Celestial Gate in token of my certain going in after it: all which things I doubt you want, and want them because you came not in at the Gate. *Christian has got his Lord's coat on his back, and is comforted therewith, he is comforted also with his mark, and his roll*

To these things they gave him no answer, only they looked upon each other, and laughed. Then I saw that they went on all, save that Christian kept before, who had no more talk but with himself, and that sometimes sighingly, and sometimes comfortably: also he would be often reading in the roll that one of the Shining Ones gave him, by which he was refreshed.

I believe then, that they all went on till they came
He comes to to the foot of a Hill, at the bottom of which was a
the Hill spring. There was also in the same place two other
Difficulty ways besides that which came straight from the Gate;
one turned to the left hand, and the other to the right,
at the bottom of the Hill: but the narrow way lay
right up the Hill (and the name of the going up the
side of the Hill is called Difficulty). Christian now
went to the spring and drank thereof to refresh himself, and then began to go up the Hill, saying,

This Hill, though high, I covet to ascend,
The difficulty will not me offend,
For I perceive the way to life lies here;
Come, pluck up, heart; let's neither faint nor fear:
Better, though difficult, the right way to go,
Than wrong, though easy, where the end is woe.

The other two also came to the foot of the Hill. But
when they saw that the Hill was steep and high, and
that there was two other ways to go; and supposing
also that these two ways might meet again with that
up which Christian went, on the other side of the
Hill; therefore they were resolved to go in those
ways. (Now the name of one of those ways was
Danger, and the name of the other Destruction.)
The danger So the one took the way which is called Danger,
of turning out which led him into a great wood, and the other took
of the way directly up the way to Destruction, which led him
into a wide field full of dark mountains,[39] where he
stumbled and fell, and rose no more.

I looked then after Christian, to see him go up the
Hill, where I perceived he fell from running to going,
and from going to clambering upon his hands and
his knees, because of the steepness of the place. Now
Award of about the midway to the top of the Hill was a
grace pleasant Arbour, made by the Lord of the Hill, for

the refreshing of weary travellers. Thither therefore
Christian got, where also he sat down to rest him.
Then he pulled his roll out of his bosom, and read
therein to his comfort; he also now began afresh to
take a review of the coat or garment that was given
him as he stood by the Cross. Thus pleasing himself
a while, he at last fell into a slumber, and thence into
a fast sleep, which detained him in that place until it
was almost night, and in his sleep his roll fell out of *He that sleeps*
his hand. Now as he was sleeping, there came one *is a loser*
to him and awaked him, saying 'Go to the ant, thou
sluggard, consider her ways, and be wise,'[40] and with that
Christian suddenly started up, and sped him on his
way, and went apace till he came to the top of the
Hill.

Now when he was got up to the top of the Hill,
there came two men running against him amain;
the name of the one was Timorous, and the name of *Christian*
the other Mistrust. To whom Christian said, 'Sirs, *meets with*
what's the matter you run the wrong way?' Timorous *Mistrust and*
answered that they were going to the City of Sion, *Timorous*
and had got up that difficult place; 'But,' said he,
'the further we go, the more danger we meet with,
wherefore we turned, and are going back again.'

'Yes,' said Mistrust, 'for just before us lie a couple
of lions in the way, whether sleeping or waking we
know not and we could not think, if we came within
reach, but they would presently pull us in pieces.'

Christian. Then said Christian, You make me afraid,
but whither shall I fly to be safe? If I go back to mine
own country, that is prepared for fire and brimstone,
and I shall certainly perish there. If I can get to the
Celestial City, I am sure to be in safety there. I must *Christian*
venture: to go back is nothing but death, to go *shakes off fear*
forward is fear of death, and life everlasting beyond
it. I will yet go forward. So Mistrust and Timorous

87

ran down the Hill, and Christian went on his way. But thinking again of what he heard from the men, he felt in his bosom for his roll[41] that he might read *Christian* therein and be comforted; but he felt, and found it *missed his roll,* not. Then was Christian in great distress, and knew *wherein he* not what to do, for he wanted that which used to *used to take* relieve him, and that which should have been his *comfort* pass into the Celestial City. Here therefore he began *He is* to be much perplexed, and knew not what to do; at *perplexed* last he bethought himself that he had slept in the *for his roll* Arbour that is on the side of the Hill: and falling down upon his knees, he asked God forgiveness for that his foolish fact,[42] and then went back to look for his roll. But all the way he went back, who can sufficiently set forth the sorrow of Christian's heart? Sometimes he sighed, sometimes he wept, and oftentimes he chid himself, for being so foolish to fall asleep in that place which was erected only for a little refreshment from his weariness. Thus therefore he went back, carefully looking on this side and on that, all the way as he went, if happily he might find his roll, that had been his comfort so many times in his journey. He went thus till he came again within sight of the Arbour, where he sat and slept; but that *Christian* sight renewed his sorrow the more, by bringing *bewails his* again, even afresh, his evil of sleeping unto his mind. *foolish* Thus therefore he now went on, bewailing his sinful *sleeping* sleep, saying, 'O wretched man that I am, that I should sleep in the day-time! That I should sleep in the midst of difficulty! That I should so indulge the flesh as to use that rest for ease to my flesh which the Lord of the Hill hath erected only for the relief of the spirits of pilgrims! How many steps have I took in vain! (Thus it happened to Israel for their sin, they were sent back again by the way of the Red Sea.)

And I am made to tread those steps with sorrow which I might have trod with delight, had it not been for this sinful sleep. How far might I have been on my way by this time! I am made to tread those steps thrice over which I needed not to have trod but once: Yea, now also I am like to be benighted, for the day is almost spent. O that I had not slept!' Now by this time he was come to the Arbour again, where for a while he sat down and wept, but at last (as Christian would have it) looking sorrowfully down under the settle, there he espied his roll; the which he with trembling and haste catched up, and put it into his bosom; but who can tell how joyful this man was, when he had gotten his roll again! For this roll was the assurance of his life, and acceptance at the desired haven. Therefore he laid it up in his bosom, gave thanks to God for directing his eye to the place where it lay, and with joy and tears betook himself again to his journey. But oh how nimbly now did he go up the rest of the Hill! Yet before he got up, the sun went down upon Christian; and this made him again recall the vanity of his sleeping to his remembrance, and thus he again began to condole with himself: 'Ah thou sinful sleep! How for thy sake am I like to be benighted in my journey! I must walk without the sun, darkness must cover the path of my feet, and I must hear the noise of doleful creatures, because of my sinful sleep!' Now also he remembered the story that Mistrust and Timorous told him of, how they were frighted with the sight of the lions. Then said Christian to himself again, 'These beasts range in the night for their prey, and if they should meet with me in the dark, how should I shift them? How should I escape being by them torn in pieces? Thus he went on his way, but while he was thus bewailing his unhappy miscarriage, he lift

Christian findeth his roll where he lost it

up his eyes, and behold there was a very stately palace before him, the name whereof was Beautiful,[43] and it stood just by the highway side.

So I saw in my dream that he made haste and went forward, that if possible he might get lodging there. Now before he had gone far, he entered into a very narrow passage, which was about a furlong off of the porter's lodge, and looking very narrowly before him as he went, he espied two lions[44] in the way. Now, thought he, I see the dangers that Mistrust and Timorous were driven back by (the lions were chained, but he saw not the chains). Then he was afraid, and thought also himself to go back after them, for he thought nothing but death was before him. But the porter at the lodge, whose name is Watchful, perceiving that Christian made a halt, as if he would go back, cried unto him saying, 'Is thy strength so small? Fear not the lions, for they are chained, and are placed there for trial of faith where it is; and for discovery of those that have none: keep in the midst of the path, and no hurt shall come unto thee.'

Then I saw that he went on, trembling for fear of the lions, but taking good heed to the directions of the porter; he heard them roar, but they did him no harm. Then he clapped his hands, and went on till he came and stood before the gate where the porter was. Then said Christian to the porter, 'Sir, what House is this? and may I lodge here tonight?' The porter answered, 'This House was built by the Lord of the Hill, and he built it for the relief and security of pilgrims.' The porter also asked whence he was, and whither he was going.

Christian. I am come from the City of Destruction, and am going to Mount Sion; but because the sun is now set, I desire, if I may, to lodge here tonight.

Porter. What is your name?

Christian. My name is, now, Christian; but my name at the first was Graceless; I came of the race of Japhet, whom God will persuade to dwell in the tents of Shem.

Porter. But how doth it happen that you come so late? The sun is set.

Christian. I had been here sooner, but that, wretched man that I am! I slept in the Arbour that stands on the hillside; nay, I had notwithstanding that, been here much sooner, but that in my sleep I lost my evidence, and came without it to the brow of the Hill; and then feeling for it, and finding it not, I was forced with sorrow of heart, to go back to the place where I slept my sleep, where I found it, and now I am come.

Porter. Well, I will call out one of the virgins of this place, who will, if she likes your talk, bring you in to the rest of the family, according to the rules of the House. So Watchful the porter rang a bell, at the sound of which came out at the door of the House, a grave and beautiful damsel named Discretion, and asked why she was called.

The porter answered, 'This man is in a journey from the City of Destruction to Mount Sion, but being weary and benighted, he asked me if he might lodge here tonight; so I told him I would call for thee, who after discourse had with him, mayest do as seemeth thee good, even according to the law of the house.'

Then she asked him whence he was, and whither he was going, and he told her. She asked him also, how he got into the way and he told her. Then she asked him what he had seen, and met with in the way, and he told her; and last, she asked his name, so he said, 'It is Christian; and I have so much the more a desire to lodge here tonight, because, by what I perceive, this place was built by the Lord of the Hill for the relief and security of pilgrims.' So she smiled, but the water stood in her eyes. And after a little pause, she said, 'I will call forth two or three more of the family.' So she ran to the door, and called out Prudence, Piety and Charity,[45] who after a little more discourse with him, had him in to the family; and many of them meeting him at the threshold of the House, said, 'Come in thou blessed of the Lord; this House was built by the Lord of the Hill on purpose to entertain such pilgrims in.' Then he bowed his head, and followed them into the House. So when he was come in, and set down, they gave him something to drink; and consented together that until supper was ready, some one or two of them should have some particular discourse with Christian, for the best improvement of time: and they appointed Piety and Prudence and Charity to discourse with him; and thus they began.

Piety. Come, good Christian, since we have been so loving to you, to receive you in to our House this night; let us, if perhaps we may better ourselves thereby, talk with you of all things that have happened to you in your pilgrimage.

Christian. With a very good will, and I am glad that you are so well disposed.

Piety. What moved you at first to betake yourself to a pilgrim's life?

Christian. I was driven out of my native country by a dreadful sound that was in mine ears, to wit, that unavoidable destruction did attend me, if I abode in that place where I was.

Piety. But how did it happen that you came out of your country this way?

Christian. It was as God would have it; for when

Piety discourses him (margin note)

How Christian was driven out of his own country (margin note)

I was under the fears of destruction I did not know whither to go; but by chance there came a man, even to me (as I was trembling and weeping), whose name is Evangelist, and he directed me to the *How he got* Wicket Gate, which else I should never have found; *into the way* and so set me into the way that hath led me directly *to Sion* to this House.

Piety. But did you not come by the House of the Interpreter?

Christian. Yes, and did see such things there, the remembrance of which will stick by me as long as I live; specially three things; to wit, how Christ, in *A rehearsal* despite of Satan, maintains his work of grace in the *of what he saw* heart; how the man had sinned himself quite out of *in the way* hopes of God's mercy; and also the dream of him that thought in his sleep the Day of Judgement was come.

Piety. Why? Did you hear him tell his dream?

Christian. Yes, and a dreadful one it was, I thought. It made my heart ache as he was telling of it, but yet I am glad I heard it.

Piety. Was that all that you saw at the House of the Interpreter?

Christian. No, he took me and had me where he showed me a stately palace, and how the people were clad in gold that were in it; and how there came a venturous man, and cut his way through the armed men that stood in the door to keep him out; and how he was bid to come in, and win eternal glory. Methought those things did ravish my heart; I could have stayed at that good man's House a twelve-month, but that I knew I had further to go.

Piety. And what saw you else in the way?

Christian. Saw! Why, I went but a little further, and I saw one, as I thought in my mind, hang bleeding upon the tree; and the very sight of him made

93

my burden fall off my back (for I groaned under a weary burden), but then it fell down from off me. 'Twas a strange thing to me, for I never saw such a thing before: Yea, and while I stood looking up (for then I could not forbear looking), three Shining Ones came to me: one of them testified that my sins were forgiven me: another stripped me of my rags, and gave me this broidered coat which you see; and the third set the mark which you see on my forehead, and gave me this sealed roll (and with that he plucked it out of his bosom).

Piety. But you saw more than this, did you not?

Christian. The things that I have told you were the best: yet some other matters I saw, as namely I saw three men, Simple, Sloth, and Presumption, lie asleep a little out of the way as I came, with irons upon their heels; but do you think I could awake them! I also saw Formalist and Hypocrisy come tumbling over the wall, to go, as they pretended, to Sion, but they were quickly lost; even as I myself did tell them, but they would not believe: but, above all, I found it hard work to get up this Hill, and as hard to come by the lions' mouths, and truly if it had not been for the good man, the porter that stands at the gate, I do not know but that after all, I might have gone back again: but now I thank God I am here, and I thank you for receiving of me.

Prudence discourses him　Then Prudence thought good to ask him a few questions, and desired his answer to them.

Prudence. Do you not think sometimes of the country from whence you came?

Christian's thoughts of his native country　*Christian*. Yes, but with much shame and detestation; *Truly, if I had been mindful of that country from whence I came out, I might have had opportunity to have returned; but now I desire a better country; that is, an heavenly.*

94

Prudence. Do you not yet bear away with you some of the things that then you were conversant withal?

Christian. Yes, but greatly against my will; especially my inward and carnal cogitations with which all my countrymen, as well as myself, were delighted; but now all those things are my grief, and might I but choose mine own things I would choose never to think of those things more; but when I would be doing of that which is best, that which is worst is with me. *Christian distasted with carnal cogitations* *Christian's choice*

Prudence. Do you not find sometimes, as if those things were vanquished, which at other times are your perplexity?

Christian. Yes, but that is but seldom; but they are to me golden hours, in which such things happens to me. *Christian's golden hours*

Prudence. Can you remember by what means you find your annoyances at times as if they were vanquished?

Christian. Yes, when I think what I saw at the Cross, that will do it; and when I look upon my broidered coat, that will do it; also when I look into the roll that I carry in my bosom, that will do it; and when my thoughts wax warm about whither I am going, that will do it. *How Christian gets power against his corruptions*

Prudence. And what is it that makes you so desirous to go to Mount Sion?

Christian. Why, there I hope to see him alive, that did hang dead on the Cross; and there I hope to be rid of all those things that to this day are in me an annoyance to me; there they say there is no death, and there I shall dwell with such company as I like best. For to tell you truth, I love him, because I was by him eased of my burden, and I am weary of my inward sickness; I would fain be where I shall die no *Why Christian would be at Mount Sion* more, and with the company that shall continually

Charity discourses him cry, *Holy, Holy, Holy.*

Then said Charity to Christian, 'Have you a family? Are you a married man?'

Christian. I have a wife and four small children.[46]

Charity. And why did you not bring them along with you?

Christian's love to his wife and children *Christian.* Then Christian wept, and said, Oh how willingly would I have done it, but they were all of them utterly averse to my going on pilgrimage.

Charity. But you should have talked to them, and have endeavoured to have shown them the danger of being behind.

Christian. So I did, and told them also what God had showed to me of the destruction of our City; but I seemed to them as one that mocked, and they believed me not.

Charity. And did you pray to God that he would bless your counsel to them?

Christian. Yes, and that with much affection; for you must think that my wife and poor children were very dear unto me.

Charity. But did you tell them of your own sorrow and fear of destruction? For I suppose that destruction was visible enough to you?

Christian. Yes, over and over and over. They might Christian's fears of perishing might be read in his very countenance also see my fears in my countenance, in my tears, and also in my trembling under the apprehension of the judgement that did hang over our heads; but all was not sufficient to prevail with them to come with me.

Charity. But what could they say for themselves The cause why his wife and children did not go with him why they came not?

Christian. Why, my wife was afraid of losing this world, and my children were given to the foolish delights of youth: so what by one thing, and what by another, they left me to wander in this manner alone.

Charity. But did you not with your vain life, damp all that you by words used by way of persuasion to bring them away with you?

Christian. Indeed I cannot commend my life; for I am conscious to myself of many failings: therein, I know also that a man by his conversation, may soon overthrow what by argument or persuasion he doth labour to fasten upon others for their good. Yet, this I can say, I was very wary of giving them occasion, by any unseemly action, to make them averse to going on pilgrimage. Yea, for this very thing, they would tell me I was too precise, and that I denied myself of things (for their sakes) in which they saw no evil. Nay, I think I may say, that, if what they saw in me did hinder them, it was my great tenderness in sinning against God, or of doing any wrong to my neighbour. *Christian's good conversation before his wife and children*

Charity. Indeed Cain hated his brother, because his own works were evil, and his brother's righteous; and if thy wife and children have been offended with thee for this they thereby show themselves to be implacable to good; and thou hast delivered thy soul from their blood. *Christian clear of their blood if they perish*

Now I saw in my dream that thus they sat talking together until supper was ready. So when they had made ready they sat down to meat. Now the table was furnished with fat things and with wine that was well refined, and all their talk at the table was about the Lord of the Hill; as namely about what he had done, and wherefore he did what he did, and why he had builded that House; and by what they said I perceived that he had been a great warrior, and had fought with and slain him that had the power of death, but not without great danger to himself, which made me love him the more. *What Christian had to his supper. Their talk at supper-time*

97

For, as they said, and as I believe (said Christian), he did it with the loss of much blood; but that which put glory of grace into all he did was, that he did it of pure love to his country. And besides, there were some of them of the household that said they had seen, and spoke with him since he did die on the Cross; and they have attested that they had it from his own lips, that he is such a lover of poor pilgrims that the like is not to be found from the east to the west.

They moreover gave an instance of what they affirmed, and that was: he had stripped himself of his glory that he might do this for the poor; and that they heard him say and affirm that he would not dwell in the Mountain of Sion alone. They said *Christ makes* moreover that he had made many pilgrims princes *princes of* though by nature they were beggars born, and their *beggars* original had been the dunghill.

Thus they discoursed together till late at night; and after they had committed themselves to their Lord for protection, they betook themselves to rest. *Christian's* The pilgrim they laid in a large upper chamber, *bed-chamber* whose window opened towards the sun rising; the name of the chamber was Peace, where he slept till break of day; and then he awoke and sang,

> *Where am I now? Is this the love and care*
> *Of Jesus, for the men that pilgrims are?*
> *Thus to provide ! That I should be forgiven !*
> *And dwell already the next door to Heaven.*

So in the morning they all got up, and after some more discourse they told him that he should not *Christian* depart, till they had showed him the rarities of that *had into the* place. And first they had him into the study where *study, and* *what he saw* they showed him records of the greatest antiquity; *there* in which, as I remember my dream, they showed him

98

first the pedigree of the Lord of the Hill, that he was the Son of the Ancient of Days, and came by an eternal generation. Here also was more fully recorded the acts that he had done, and the names of many hundreds that he had taken into his service; and how he had placed them in such habitations that could neither by length of days, nor decays of nature, be dissolved.

Then they read to him some of the worthy acts that some of his servants had done, as how they had subdued kingdoms, wrought righteousness, obtained promises, stopped the mouths of lions, quenched the violence of fire, escaped the edge of the sword, out of weakness were made strong, waxed valiant in fight, and turned to flight the armies of the aliens.

Then they read again in another part of the records of the House where it was showed how willing their Lord was to receive into his favour any, even any, though they in time past had offered great affronts to his person and proceedings. Here also were several other histories of many other famous things; of all which Christian had a view, as of things both ancient and modern, together with prophecies and predictions of things that have their certain accomplishment, both to the dread and amazement of enemies, and the comfort and solace of pilgrims.

The next day they took him, and had him into the armoury,[47] where they showed him all manner of furniture, which their Lord had provided for pilgrims, as sword, shield, helmet, breastplate, All-Prayer, and shoes that would not wear out. And there was here enough of this, to harness out as many men for the service of their Lord as there be stars in the heaven for multitude. *Christian had into the armoury*

They also showed him some of the engines with which some of his servants had done wonderful

99

Christian is made to see ancient things things. They showed him Moses' rod, the hammer and nail with which Jael slew Sisera, the pitchers, trumpets, and lamps too, with which Gideon put to flight the armies of Midian. Then they showed him the ox's goad wherewith Shamger slew six hundred men. They showed him also the jaw-bone with which Sampson did such mighty feats; they showed him moreover the sling and stone with which David slew Goliah of Gath: and the sword also with which their Lord will kill the man of sin, in the day that he shall rise up to the prey. They showed him besides many excellent things, with which Christian was much delighted. This done, they went to their rest again.

Then I saw in my dream, that on the morrow he got up to go forwards, but they desired him to stay till the next day also. 'And then,' said they, 'we will *Christian showed the Delectable Mountains* (if the day be clear) show you the Delectable Mountains,'[48] which they said would yet further add to his comfort, because they were nearer the desired haven than the place where at present he was. So he consented and stayed. When the morning was up they had him to the top of the House, and bid him look south; so he did, and behold, at a great distance he saw a most pleasant mountainous country, beautified with woods, vineyards, fruits of all sorts; flowers also, with springs and fountains, very delectable to behold. Then he asked the name of the country; they said it was Immanuel's Land: 'And it is as common,' said they, 'as this Hill is to and for all the pilgrims. And when thou comest there, from thence, thou mayest see to the Gate of the Celestial City, as the shepherds that live there will make appear.

Christian sets forward Now he bethought himself of setting forward, and they were willing he should: 'But first,' said they, 'let us go again into the armoury'; so they did; and

when he came there, they harnessed him from head *Christian*
to foot with what was of proof, lest perhaps he should *sent away*
meet with assaults in the way. He being therefore *armed*
thus accoutred walketh out with his friends to the
gate, and there he asked the porter if he saw any
pilgrims pass by; then the porter answered, 'Yes.'

Charity. Pray, did you know him?

Porter. I asked his name, and he told me it was
Faithful.

Christian. O, said Christian, I know him, he is my
townsman, my near neighbour, he comes from the
place where I was born: how far do you think he may
be before?

Porter. He is got by this time below the Hill.

Christian. Well, said Christian, good porter, the *How*
Lord be with thee, and add to all thy blessings much *Christian*
increase, for the kindness that thou hast showed to *and the porter*
greet at
me. *parting*

Then he began to go forward, but Discretion,
Piety, Charity, and Prudence would accompany him
down to the foot of the Hill. So they went on together, reiterating their former discourses till they
came to go down the Hill. Then said Christian, 'As
it was difficult coming up, so (so far as I can see) it is
dangerous going down.' 'Yes,' said Prudence, 'so it
is; for it is an hard matter for a man to go down into
the Valley of Humiliation, as thou art now, and to
catch no slip by the way; therefore,' said they, 'are
we come out to accompany thee down the Hill.'
So he began to go down, but very warily, yet he
caught a slip or two.

Then I saw in my dream that these good companions (when Christian was gone down to the
bottom of the Hill) gave him a loaf of bread, a bottle
of wine, and a cluster of raisins; and then he went on
his way.